HMS CRACKER

By the same author

Gun-Brig Captain
The Lee Shore
Stella and the Fireships
Mutiny in the Caribbean
The Malta Frigate
Seven Gun Broadside
The Quarterdeck Ladder
A Sword for Mr Fitton
Mr Fitton's Commission
The Baltic Convoy
A Kiss for Captain Hardy
Centurion Comes Home

HMS CRACKER

SHOWELL STYLES

WILLIAM KIMBER

First published in 1988

British Library Cataloguing in Publication data

Styles, Showell, *1908-*
H.M.S. Cracker
I. Title
823'.914 [F]

ISBN 0-7183-0700-3

William Kimber & Co Ltd is part of the Thorsons Publishing Group, Wellingborough, Northamptonshire, NN8 2RQ, England.

Photoset in North Wales by
Derek Doyle & Associates Mold, Clwyd
and Printed in Great Britain by
Biddles Limited, Guildford, Surrey

1 3 5 7 9 10 8 6 4 2

Contents

[illegible]

The tides of [illegible] for [illegible]
appointed [illegible] the [illegible]
to flow of [illegible]
mid-afternoon [illegible] day [illegible]
his rum [illegible]
that if he could [illegible] the [illegible]
done. Then [illegible] as [illegible]
with Shakespeare [illegible] should [illegible]
about sorrow [illegible] not [illegible]

The morning [illegible]
stration of [illegible]
ished re[illegible]
comp[illegible]
with the [illegible]
taken until [illegible]
seven [illegible] Re[illegible]
four adoring [illegible] pu[illegible]
years at least [illegible] hea[illegible]
Cecilia [illegible] able
of the [illegible] be
had paid [illegible] call
sweetness [illegible] the de[illegible]
Mrs Cecilia was [illegible]
than himself [illegible]
sweetness [illegible]

I

Sea of Troubles

1

The tide of trouble for Henry Honeyburn, newly-appointed captain of His Majesty's gun-brig *Cracker*, began to flow on the fourteenth of August in the year 1813. By mid-afternoon of that day, standing drenched to the skin on his rain-swept quarterdeck, Honeyburn was telling himself that if he could pass this present crisis safely the Fates had done their worst. As an ex-schoolmaster well acquainted with Shakespeare, he should have remembered the lines about sorrows coming not in single spies but in battalions.

The morning had been bad enough, with a demonstration of his own shameful cowardice. *Cracker* had finished refitting and was ready for sailing with the Spanish convoy on the 15th, so on the previous evening Honeyburn, with the sudden decision that was characteristic of him, had taken an illicit twelve hours' leave of absence and ridden the seven miles to Wickham Rectory and the welcome of his four adoring sisters. His purpose (in mind for the past five years at least) was to lay heart and hand at the feet of Mrs Cecilia Tuftoe, a personable widow who had been a friend of the Honeyburns since they were all children together. He had paid his morning call – a dish of tea, Mrs Cecilia sweetness itself – but the declaration had not been made. Mrs Cecilia was nearing middle-age, a year or two younger than himself; she was well-to-do and shrewd despite her sweetness. She would see him for what he was, he told himself – an ageing lieutenant with little or no prospect of advancement in his profession, a captain only by courtesy (for a gun-brig was a lieutenant's command) and liable to be put ashore on half-pay at a whim of Admiralty. She might think he was after her money. She might very well refuse him. He had gulped his tea, stammered polite adieux, and mounted his hired nag to ride back to Portsmouth.

A mile short of Southwick the hack cast a shoe and there was an hour's delay at the forge while she was reshod. Blustery rain-squalls drove in his face as he came down into the town and returned his mount to the livery stables. By ill luck the first person he encountered when he hurried through the gates onto the Common Hard was Page, port captain, who returned his salute with an oath and a popeyed glare.

'Where the devil have you been, Mr Honeyburn?' Page demanded loudly. 'By God, I'll take order with you, sir! Here's your vessel over at Daneman's Wharf since daybreak and not a commissioned officer aboard her.'

'Daneman's Wharf, sir?'

'That's what I said, sir! They're dismounting your bow-chasers, remounting one as stern-chaser, prigging t'other. You'll be lucky if the thieving bastards don't prig your carronades too, when you're not there to watch 'em,' Captain Page added venomously.

He was short and fat in marked contrast to the lieutenant's gaunt six-foot-two. A pair of dockyard mateys shambling past with a ladder were much amused. Honeyburn was aghast. His cherished long six-pounders – the guns he and his late captain Michael Fitton had won for *Cracker* after heaven alone knew what amount of cajolery and bribery!

'They can't take her bow-chasers!' he stammered.

'They can and will,' said the port captain shortly. 'Admiralty order brought by some jumped-up jack-in-office from the Ordnance Board –' he caught himself up. 'That's by the way. You'll get over there this instant, Mr Honeyburn, and you'll bring her back to moorings yourself.

I won't have vessels sculling about in this harbour with no one but warrant officers in charge.'

'I beg your pardon, sir,' Honeyburn said stiffly. 'As you are aware, I still await the appointment of a first lieutenant to *Cracker*. Had I known –'

'Yes, yes, yes. You'll hear something as to that before the day is out. I had a signal this morning. Etheridge? Yes, Etheridge was the name. If a Mr Etheridge comes aboard you, Honeyburn, you'll be good enough to treat him with respect.' Page allowed himself a sour grin. 'He's – you might say – very well-connected.'

'Aye aye, sir. But may I ask –'

'Hell and damnation!' A gust of wind and rain lifted Page's cocked hat from his head and he caught it just in time. 'See to it, Mr Honeyburn – and take notice that there's a convoy conference on board *Crane* at four bells of the first dog. You will not fail to attend it.'

He trotted away in the direction of the port offices. Honeyburn hurried across the Hard to the quay and found a wherry. Twenty minutes later he was climbing aboard the vessel that had been his home for the past three years. He cut short the chorus of explanation from his three warrant officers – Mr Sholto the boatswain, Mr Trapp the carpenter, and Mr Grattan the cook – and stalked aft. Daneman's had finished the job. One of his long sixes was a stern-chaser now and the other was gone – *Cracker* had no bow-chaser and his theory of naval gunnery, which had proved its worth in the fight with the American privateer *Lexington* only last month, could no longer be applied in practice. From the imperturbable Lieutenant Fitton, whom he had greatly admired, Honeyburn had learned to conceal his emotions, and his high-pitched voice giving the orders to cast-off and make sail gave no hint of his anger and frustration. Angry and frustrated he was, however, and (with this morning's events fresh in his mind) bitterly conscious of his own shortcomings. Five minutes after leaving Daneman's Wharf these feelings were swept away by the worst squall of that unseasonable August day.

It came driving in from Spithead from due south, charging across the two-mile breadth of Portsmouth Harbour and setting the multitude of ships lurching and reeling at their moorings. Despite the double-reefed topsails which were all the canvas *Cracker* carried on her two tall masts she scudded along with a bone in her teeth, chasing the ever-receding curtain of heavy rain that hid everything ahead of her except a hundred yards of wind-whipped water. And if acute apprehensiveness is equivalent to fear, then her captain was afraid.

Less than eight weeks ago Lieutenant Honeyburn, busy at his beloved bow-chasers, had not turned a hair when the balls of *Lexington*'s broadside had whistled past his ears; he had made guns and gunnery his study and he knew what he was doing. But this was different. For one thing, it was the first time he had taken charge of *Cracker* under sail with sole responsibility for her, for since he had been appointed to command her in place of Fitton she had been at moorings or alongside. For another, and more significantly, he knew he was no seaman and never would be one. He had scraped through the theoretical seamanship at his examination for lieutenant, he was adequately efficient as a deck officer, he had learned enough in his three years with Michael Fitton to handle a ship in moderate weather when he had plenty of sea-room. But he lacked the close affinity with the sea that men like Fitton possessed and which seemed to Honeyburn a sixth sense, the special sensibility that received communication from every circumstance of a ship at sea – the look and motion of sea and cloud, the changing voice of the wind, the variation in the tremor of the deck underfoot. Without that sensibility, he told himself guiltily, he had no business to be in charge of a vessel under sail.

Honeyburn was standing a little abaft the man at the wheel, hands behind back, the rain that was soaking his blue coat spouting intermittently from his cocked hat. His long bony face, tanned to parchment-colour rather than a sailorlike brown, showed nothing of his inner uncertainty.

He stole a quick glance at the men on deck: Sholto the boatswain, his red hair plastered across his glistening face, was buttoning the collar of his pea-jacket a couple of paces away; for'ard along the deck the seamen of the duty watch were chatting and laughing as they squatted in the lee of the canvas-hooded carronades.

Peters, the big seaman at the helm, had apparently no doubt at all that he was steering the right course for *Cracker*'s mooring at number twenty-two buoy, west. Honeyburn had plenty of doubts. There was four square miles of harbour water, it was true, but it held hundreds of ships of all sizes, most of them alongside at quays and wharves but scores of them at moorings. Three 74's, he recalled, were moored in line – they would be right athwart the gun-brig's present course. He strained his sight to pierce the silver curtain of rain. Huge grey shapes loomed and darkened, the double rows of gunports grew suddenly plain. *Cracker*, with the wind just abaft the beam, would never clear the outermost ship; he would have to wear on the other tack.

He had opened his mouth to give the order when Sholto cleared his throat and spoke as if to himself.

'Neat an' handy, that is. Gives us a pistol-shot clearance of *Indomitable*'s buoy.'

Honeyburn closed his mouth. And Sholto was right, of course. The gun-brig sped past well clear of the buoy, half a cable-length from the 74's towering bows and massive bowsprit; had he followed his impulse and sheered away on the opposite tack they would have been next-door to lost in this impenetrable maze of rain whereas they were on course still and now within minutes of their objective.

A small cutter, close-hauled and heeled far over, shot across *Cracker*'s bows twenty fathoms away and vanished again into the rain. But the rain was thinning, the squall blowing itself out. Up in the receding whiteness ahead bars of blurred green showed – there was sunshine there on Ports Down – and suddenly two moored vessels with an empty space between them were revealed right ahead. That was *Cracker*'s mooring, between the *Wolverine* bark and the 18-gun brig-sloop *Crane*; and now he had to face the business of picking up moorings. If only he had a second-in-command, a first lieutenant, he could with fair excuse leave the operation to him. Yet he had done it often when Fitton had been giving the orders, and it was simple enough in all conscience – or would be if it wasn't for the squally wind.

Honeyburn glanced quickly round him, noting the boat ready for hoisting outboard, the crew standing by, the cable flaked-down for veering. His glance went to the rapidly-approaching mooring. He had to gauge an exact distance, an exact moment, to ensure that when *Cracker* came to the wind the cable could be taken to the buoy before she had time to drift stern-first onto *Crane*. He took a deep breath.

'Bear away half-a-point, Peters.' He felt rather than saw the boatswain's approving jerk of the head. 'Now – helm a-weather, hard over.'

Cracker heeled as she swept round to starboard into the gap. He hesitated, trying to estimate wind-force and the gun-brig's slackening speed. Sholto cleared his throat with a sound like the fall of Babel and instantly Honeyburn's shrill tenor rose in sharp orders.

'Sheets, there – back the fore-tops'l! Boat away! Lively, now!'

It was a sufficiently neat piece of work, and in five minutes *Cracker* was lying comfortably to her buoy with the hands taking in her canvas. Her captain concealed his great relief as best he could, but his voice as he told the boatswain to make all snug and have a boat ready for him in fifty-five minutes' time held a perceptible tremor. He went below to his cabin in a dismal mood. The faint satisfaction at having brought off a piece of primary seamanship without mishap, at having turned aside at least one of the arrows (he trusted it was the last) that Fate was aiming at him on this disastrous day, was banished by the knowledge that he had been wholly dependent on Sholto for its success. He had stripped off his drenched coat when a knock on the cabin door heralded the entrance of Shorty Band with a steaming mug of coffee. Hezekiah Band, nearly as broad as he was tall, had constituted himself captain's steward in Fitton's time.

''Ere we are, sir,' he said cheerfully. 'Best get this down you afore you casts off them wet duds. There was an orficer in the old *Mediator*, much o' your build 'e was, what took a chill as brought on a low fever –'

'Very well, Band.'

Honeyburn dismissed him with a nod and a frown. Ordinarily it would have been thanks and a smile, for he had the foible (for foible it was in a naval lieutenant) of regarding the hands as human beings with feelings, like himself. But the little man's prompt attention was merely another weight to lower his present depression. They were coddling him, he reflected gloomily as he sipped the scalding coffee; treating him like a senile invalid, a feeble incompetent. And there was justification here, for compared with *Cracker*'s former captain he *was* incompetent. Fitton would somehow have brought his crew up to complement by now but his own pleas to the Quota Office had so far brought him nothing; instead of the crew of fifty he should have had the gun-brig numbered only thirty-eight seamen and two boys. And Fitton, he was sure, would have contrived to keep those bow-chasers.

He drained the mug and groped in his locker for dry clothing. The coffee was beginning to take effect and his spirits rose a little. At least the remainder of the day offered no problems or hazards that he could not cope with. There was the convoy conference aboard *Crane*, a formality concerned mainly with confirming signals and order of sailing at which he would have to do little but sit and listen. The convoy consisted of three big transports crammed with troops for Lord Wellington's army on the Peninsula, and it was to be escorted by *Crane*, 18-gun brig-sloop, and the smaller *Cracker*, sailing tomorrow afternoon for Wellington's latest supply-port of Orio.

Except for her reduced crew, *Cracker* was fully ready for sea; and unless they ran into unseasonable weather in the Bay Honeyburn felt he could creditably manage a voyage he had made five times already under Fitton's captaincy. He would have the assistance of a lieutenant, too, if the port captain was to be believed.

Honeyburn, by now in his best uniform coat and clean white trousers, took the muster-book from the shelf and sat at his little table under the dim light of the small glazed port. He did not at once open the book but sat staring at the bulkhead considering Captain Page's somewhat obscure announcement. What sort of man would this Etheridge – if that was his name – turn out to be? This last-minute appointment meant that he would have little time to discover his efficiency or otherwise before *Cracker* sailed, or to establish the peculiar relationship that had to be formed between two officers of equal rank one of whom was totally subordinate to the other. For months ahead this stranger was to be the nearest approach to a companion, a confidant, that he as captain could have. What had Page meant by his adjuration to 'treat him with respect' and his remark that Etheridge was very well connected?

As he pondered frowning, Honeyburn was aware that the thud of feet on the deck above him, the sounds of ropes being coiled-down and boat stowed, had ceased and been replaced by a faint rumble of voices from the warrant-officers' mess a few yards away below decks. There were three bulkheads in between and he could hear nothing of the words spoken; which was perhaps just as well.

In the gunroom, as the tiny cabin was meticulously called, Mr Grattan the cook was refuting the boatswain's opinion that *Cracker* would have to sail without a first lieutenant. Though rated warrant-officer cook, Grattan could hand, reef, and steer as well as any able seaman on board; he was a craggy-faced Ulsterman and inclined to be a sea-lawyer.

''Tis in King's Regulations,' he was saying. 'A gun-brig of our force can't sail from a home port without there's a pair of commissioned officers aboard her – so it's griping for naught ye are, John Sholto.'

'That's sartin sure,' agreed Mr Trapp, nodding his grey head judicially; he was the oldest man on board and regarded himself as a final authority on most things. 'We'll 'ave a Number One afore we sail. And when 'e comes, when 'e comes, I say –'

'Heard ye the first time,' muttered Grattan.

'– let's 'ope 'e's a proper seaman,' pursued the carpenter. 'Because why? Because this vessel ain't fully defective without a proper seaman on 'er quarterdeck.'

'True for ye,' nodded Grattan. 'I declare I've a liking for Honey, but there's no denying he's the spit an' image of an old woman.'

Sholto sat upright, his big weatherbeaten face stern. 'Mr Grattan,' he said slowly, 'I'll thank you to speak respectful of Mr Honeyburn. You ain't forgot how he shot the guts out of *Lexington*, I suppose?'

'He's no seaman, all the same,' Grattan said.

'You and me have served under worse captains,' the boatswain continued unheeding. 'Mr Honeyburn's a gennleman and he'll work the ship fair enough if we stand by him, first lieutenant or no first lieutenant. Carping and crabbing won't help the ship, and it's the ship that matters, right?'

They nodded assent. All three were old man-o'-war's men and this was their creed. Mr Trapp's wizened face wrinkled in thought.

'All very well, Mr Sholto,' he pronounced, 'but we 'ave 'ere a hunknown quantity – a hunknown quantity, I say. This 'ypothemical first lieutenant. Say 'e's a right seaman, one o' your 'ard-'orse men –'

He stopped as Gomez, the seaman on deck-watch, put his head into the cabin.

'Boat comin' alongside, Mr Sholto,' said Gomez. 'Gent wants a word with the cap'n – name of Etheridge.'

'I'll tell the captain,' said Sholto, getting up.

2

The name Etheridge brought Honeyburn out of a gloomy study of the muster-book and on deck in a hurry. He emerged, blinking in the bright sunshine that had succeeded the squall, just as the newcomer clambered awkwardly over the rail – awkwardly, because he was wearing a long fawn topcoat with a high roll-collar and elaborate frogging across the chest. On his head was a tall beaver hat in the latest London fashion, which he raised with some care so as not to displace the palpable wig of curly hair, an unlikely auburn, beneath it. At the same time he made a little duck of his head towards the quarterdeck, showing that he knew the correct procedure when boarding one of His Majesty's warships.

'Captain Honeyburn? Frank Etheridge, at your service, sir,' he said in a languid voice, glancing sharply all round him as he spoke.

Honeyburn was in a quandary. Never to his knowledge had a joining officer reported to his captain dressed like that.

'Er – Lieutenant Etheridge?' he ventured.

Mr Etheridge tittered. 'Lord love you, sir, do I look it?'

'I beg your pardon,' Honeyburn said stiffly. 'I am expecting an officer to join this vessel today.'

'And rightly, captain. Of that I have something to say, if –' he looked at Gomez and the boatswain, who were gazing at him admiringly from a few yards away – 'if we may be afforded some little privacy.'

'Please to come below, sir.'

Honeyburn led the way down to his cabin, cautioning his visitor to mind his head as they entered. Etheridge allowed his top-hat to be taken from him and set on a sea-chest, while his sharp eyes took in the small wooden cell and its sparse furniture – table and two chairs, locker, railed shelf of books, sword and boat-cloak depending from a hook.

'Spartan, 'pon my word,' he remarked as he sat down; he was round-faced and bulbous-nosed, and the blotched cheeks and incipient double chin suggested the *bon viveur*.

'Perhaps,' Honeyburn returned coldly, seating himself. 'Pray forgive me for mentioning that my duties require me to be aboard *Crane*, next astern, in half-an-hour's time. I can spare you twenty minutes, no more.'

Mr Etheridge tilted his head back and looked down his nose at him. 'And if I tell you, Captain Honeyburn, that I represent His Royal Highness the Prince Regent in this matter? That I was requested – nay, ordered – to make this visit to you by HRH in person?'

'I have my own orders, sir, and I obey them.'

Honeyburn's pale blue eyes could stare icily when he was much annoyed. Etheridge met them with a look unexpectedly acute and searching. Then he nodded and shrugged.

'Very well. Captain Page told you nothing of my mission?'

'He told me I was to expect you and that you were very well connected.'

'Droll fellow,' Etheridge tittered; he cocked his eye at the locker. 'You wouldn't chance to have a glass of cherry brandy in that box, captain, would you? It seems I must talk fast and it'll be demnition dry work.'

'I have some madeira.' Honeyburn took bottle and glasses from the locker and poured the wine. 'I trust it will be to your taste, sir,' he added drily.

'A right Bual,' said Etheridge, sipping. 'I prefer it to the Verdelho, though HRH will have none of it. Says it's too sweet, though how a man whose favourite tipple is cherry brandy –'

'Just so,' Honeyburn interrupted firmly. 'But I was to hear something concerning my first lieutenant, I believe.'

'Lord love you, captain, I come to it now. I abhor haste – *tempus est quaedam pars aeternitas*.'

'In my Service, sir, *tempus anima rei*.'

'And there's my cue,' Etheridge grinned. 'You, sir, are

Henry Honeyburn, Master of Arts, one-time usher at Westminster School. Your father, lately deceased – pray accept my condolences – was rector of Wickham in Hampshire and brother-in-law to Admiral Laurie. You were intended for a naval career and placed upon the ship's books of a battleship at a very early age, which I collect to be a not uncommon practice among those doting parents who have strings to pull. In the event, however, you chose to be a schoolmaster. – How, pray,' Etheridge interrupted himself, 'did you come to change your profession so late in life?'

Time flashed back to the low-ceilinged room in Chiswick Mall, Mr Coleridge reading the latest sonnet of his friend William Wordsworth: *We must be free or die, who speak the tongue That Shakespeare spake, the faith and morals hold Which Milton held –*

'I was moved to take a hand in bringing down Bonaparte, sir,' Honeyburn said distantly.

Etheridge stared, wagged his false curls. 'Re-markable, 'pon honour. However – a midshipman's berth was found for you, no doubt with some pulling of those invaluable strings, and – I cut my story short – here you are, captain of your own ship. By the bye, I gather that her former captain was reprimanded and dismissed from command. Has it never occurred to you to wonder that his first lieutenant should receive promotion?'

It had occurred to Honeyburn, as to a good many other people, but he was in no mood to admit it.

'Mr Etheridge,' he said sharply, 'I believe your question verges on impertinence, as indeed does your prying into my private life. Unless you can give me good reason for –'

'My dear captain! I intend no offence, no offence in the world. Pray indulge me – and allow me to beg for another glass. Perhaps I've erred,' Etheridge went on as Honeyburn, with no very good grace, poured the wine, 'in putting the cart before the horse, Part Two of my tale before Part One. Here now is Part One – and I trust, captain, in your treating it as particularly confidential.'

'You may do so, sir.'

'Not, however, that the exordium is anything but common knowledge. His Royal Highness the Prince Regent – Prinny, as we his intimates and servants are permitted to call him – has over the years indulged in a good many of what our enemies across the Channel call *liaisons*. Most, I fancy, he has forgotten, but one – it was nineteen years ago – lingers in his memory. At least, it recurred to him last month. Ah, memory!' Etheridge rolled his eyes and sighed sentimentally. 'The dear kind women of the past! How roseate our remembrance of them when we look back from middle-age! I dare say you find the same yourself, captain.'

'Nothing of the kind,' Honeyburn said testily. 'And I'll ask you to note that I must leave for *Crane* in ten minutes' time.'

'Then I'll cut my tale to the bare bones. There was a Kitty Muspratt – Prinny was thirty-two at the time – and he fathered her child, a boy child. Prinny being some thousands in debt at the time, no provision was made, it seems. His conscience smote him – for Prinny has both heart and conscience when he remembers 'em – and I was deputed to discover what had become of this lad. The mother, I found, had died, but not before her new protector, a naval officer, had contrived to enter her boy – at the age of nine, sir – as midshipman on board the *Carnatic* seventy-four. This I reported to Prinny. His present fancy, I must explain, is to be a man of learning, acquainted with the Classics, and he went into a tizzy about this boy's lack of proper education. Get him out of the Navy, says he, put him to school and college. I explained the difficulty, if not the impossibility, the young man having passed the examination for lieutenant three weeks ago. Then find a ship with a proper schoolmaster on board, says Prinny, and God strikes me if I don't make 'em shift him to her.'

'Good gracious!' This was Honeyburn's nearest approach to an oath. 'You don't mean to say that I'm to receive –'

'Permit me to finish, captain, since you're in a hurry. It was a fortunate meeting with Admiral Laurie that put me in possession of your own history, and it was the Admiral who mentioned the situation as regards *Cracker* – Fitton deprived of command, yourself likely to be put ashore on half-pay. Master of Arts, late Westminster School – says Prinny when I reported to him – by God, he'll stay in that ship and George shall sail with him.' Etheridge noticed Honeyburn's incredulous stare. 'Oh, these things can be arranged, captain – if you've strings enough to pull and a Prince Regent to help you pull 'em.' He finished his madeira and set down the glass. 'The Muspratt had him christened George Fitzjames, James being one of Prinny's dozen other names. And now I've obeyed my master and seen you for myself I'll send Lieutenant Fitzjames to join you, or report to you, or whatever the proper phrase is.'

'Wait!' Honeyburn said distractedly as he rose to his feet. 'Am I to understand that I'm expected to instruct this – this –'

'Royal by-blow,' Etheridge suggested.

'– To teach him Greek and Latin, in addition to my duties as captain of this ship? Let me tell you, sir, that my prime responsibility is my command, which leaves me little or no time –'

'Pray listen to me, captain. I've obeyed my orders and no doubt you'll obey yours. What time you spend on young George's education is your affair entirely – you'll get no Admiralty order concerning it. 'Tis just a matter of obliging Prinny. And between you and me –' Etheridge paused on the first step of the ladder – 'I'll lay a thousand to one he'll have forgotten it in a fortnight.'

'But this young man knows his – his origins?'

'He knows, and I'd say he don't much like 'em. Neither does he like being transferred from *Centaur* where he'd just been made fifth lieutenant. That's the sum of what I know of Mr Fitzjames after two hours' acquaintance, for he's not what you'd call a conversable lad.'

Honeyburn followed his visitor on deck with his mind in something of a whirl. He had quite forgotten his convoy meeting until Sholto, respectfully intercepting him, reported that his boat was waiting alongside. Mr Etheridge doffed his tall hat and resumed it again.

'Adieu, captain,' he said, 'and my thanks for your brief but refreshing hospitality. I go hence to the Blue Posts, where I shall direct Lieutenant Fitzjames to repair on board instanter.'

Honeyburn collected his wits. 'No, that won't serve – I shall be absent for an hour or more. Mr Fitzjames had better not report until the first watch – that is, he is not to come before eight o'clock.'

As he spoke a hand trotted past to sound two double strokes on the ship's bell. Four bells! He was late already. He saw Etheridge down the side into the boat with scant ceremony, dashed below for hat and boat-cloak, and hurled himself into the sternsheets of *Cracker*'s cockboat.

'*Crane* – and stretch out!' he snapped at the two oarsmen.

During her refit the gun-brig's complement of boats had been changed, and she now carried longboat and cutter. It was typical of Honeyburn to take the cock-boat; he saw no sense in manning the cutter to pull him a couple of hundred yards, and he had no use for show. So the cock-boat nosed in among the smart gigs of the transport captains and the port captain's barge to reach the ladder *Crane* had rigged, and Honeyburn clambered aboard in a hurry, sweating in the warmth of the summer evening. Cox, the first lieutenant, raised his eyebrows as he returned Honeyburn's salute and gestured urgently aft.

The brig-sloop was not as large as a frigate but her after-cabin was a palace compared to the captain's quarters in *Cracker*. A row of small glazed ports admitted the sunlight and there was plenty of elbow-room for the five men who sat round the table – the masters of the three transports, Captain Page, and McCormick who commanded the brig-sloop; McCormick wore a single epaulette on his left shoulder to denote his rank of master and commander. As Honeyburn sidled in through the door as unobtrusively as he could Caldecott of the *Dunsmore* transport was holding forth somewhat querulously but stopped speaking as the port captain held up a hand and fixed his pop-eyed glare on the newcomer.

'You're late, Mr Honeyburn!' rasped Page, pointing the obvious.

'I beg your pardon, sir,' Honeyburn said woodenly; he knew better than to offer excuses.

Page waved him impatiently to the vacant chair next to McCormick and addressed Caldecott.

'Your annoyance is understandable, captain, but pray remember I'm not responsible for the Army's shortcomings. By military standards there's doubtless good reason why the thirteenth and twenty-third of the line can't be got to Portsmouth for another four days.'

'A damned disgraceful muddle,' said Caldecott, a small hard-faced man with an aggressive manner. 'We were told this was a matter of extreme urgency, urged to work day and night to have all ready for the embarkation tomorrow, and now you tell us we don't sail till the eighteenth. I understood you to say that Lord Wellington – we know he's besieging San Sebastian – is in sore need of these troops.'

'Sure and he's in sore need, sir,' put in McCormick, twisting round to face him. 'Hasn't he had one slam at San Sebastian and didn't the Frogs drive him back?'

Honeyburn knew little of *Crane*'s captain, whom he had heard referred to as 'Mad McCormick,' except that he hailed (like Wellington) from Dublin and was reputed to consider himself as great an authority on the strategy of the war in the Peninsula as Wellington himself.

'Here's Soult outnumbering him on that front,' he was saying now with growing enthusiasm, his eyes agleam and a lock of black hair drooping across his forehead, 'and Clausel coming up from Pamplona – 'twas in the *Chronicle* that Clausel's at Pamplona and it's as sure as death he'll be cracking-on all sail to join Soult –'

'Very well, very well, Mr McCormick!' Page cut him short

impatiently. 'I daresay you're right but it's quite beside the present point. We're concerned here with the new orders for the Orio convoy. For Mr Honeyburn's benefit,' he went on with a scowl at the latecomer, 'I'll repeat myself. General Danvers can't get his redcoats to Portsmouth before the seventeenth. They'll embark at first light on the morning of the eighteenth and the convoy will sail before noon of that day.'

The master of the *Wilton Castle* Indiaman, a big slow-spoken man, leaned forward frowning. 'If the military have bungled it once they can do it again,' he said. 'How sure, sir, can we be of this new sailing-date?'

'You may lay your life on it, Captain Nunn,' Page returned with emphasis. 'I've seen the dispatch from the Secretary for War and you can be assured there'll be no second bungle. The Government's well aware that San Sebastian's a key fortress and must be taken.'

'Aye – the key to France,' McCormick muttered aside to Honeyburn; he sat up suddenly and looked at the port captain. 'The *Caroline*, sir –'

'Yes, yes – that's been thought of,' Page snapped. 'The sloop *Caroline*, gentlemen, sailed two days ago for Orio with dispatches apprising Lord Wellington of when he might expect these reinforcements. That information's now superseded and it's been decided that he must be informed of the new arrival date as soon as possible. Dispatches are being sent post from London and *Cracker* – the speediest craft we have at hand – will sail for Orio with them tomorrow. You're ready for sea, I take it?' he added with a glare at Honeyburn.

'Yes, sir. I regret to add that I am still a dozen hands below complement.'

'Then why the devil haven't you –' Page checked himself; there were merchant captains present. 'You'll have to sail short. Your new lieutenant has reported?'

'He's to come on board this evening, sir.'

'Well, these dispatches should arrive by mid afternoon

and you can sail on the afternoon tide. Given reasonable weather you should make the passage in five days. The message you carry is of importance, Mr Honeyburn, and you'll use every effort to reach Orio by the twenty-first.'

'Aye, aye, sir,' said Honeyburn, feigning confidence but thinking of the tricky seas off Ushant and the unpredictable Bay.

Thatcher of the *Good Report*, a leather-faced old seaman who had not so far spoken, nodded a grizzled head.

'You'll do it, sir,' he croaked. 'A westerly followed by southerly squalls – seen it a dozen times. Now she'll back easterly and stay there. Sweet sailing down-channel 'twould have been for us, captain, if you'd kept to the date you told us.'

'Well, it's no fault of mine,' Page said irritably. 'Now, gentlemen. The convoy order and signals still stand but we'll meet to confirm them on the seventeenth – here on board *Crane*, Mr McCormick, with your leave.'

'Of course, sir.'

'Then since we have nothing further to discuss there's no point in prolonging this meeting.'

Page started to get up but sat down again reluctantly as Caldecott spoke in his rasping voice.

'Wait a bit. There's the matter of our escort. We haven't heard who's to take *Cracker*'s place.'

'There's no replacement,' Page said shortly. 'You'll have *Crane* and the Admiral considers she's sufficient escort.'

'Then I must beg the Admiral's leave to differ,' said Caldecott. 'An eighteen-gun vessel and a gun-brig were little enough escort for a convoy of this importance and now we're deprived of the gun-brig. A frigate should replace her.'

He looked at his fellow-captains, who pursed their lips and nodded agreement. Captain Page shrugged his shoulders and sighed noisily.

'Captain Caldecott, you know as well as I do that a frigate is altogether out of the question. There's one only, *Princess*

Charlotte, on the Spanish station and she's fully occupied on escort duty between Corunna and Lord Wellington's other supply ports. *Thalia* won't be ready for sea for a month, the seventy-fours out yonder are awaiting refit, and every other ship of force we have is either with the blockading squadrons or patrolling on the other side of the Atlantic. If it wasn't for this damned war with America – but leave all that to one side and what have you gentlemen got to fear? The French can't get out to hurt you, and as for any *chasse-marée* that might slip out of their Channel ports – well, McCormick can deal smartly with a *chasse-marée*, as he's already shown. Eh, Mr McCormick?'

'I'll not deny it, sir. Still and on, there's another possible source of danger –'

'American privateers,' Caldecott took him up. 'I've heard they mount eighteen-pounder carronades.'

'And they took and burned *Amelia* and *Stamford* of the Santander convoy in June,' added Nunn.

Page waved a hand. 'Oh, if that's your trouble I can set your minds at rest. There's been no report of these Yankee pirates in the Bay since *Lexington* was sunk, and that was eight weeks ago. No, gentlemen –' he rose to his feet – 'there'll be no excitement of that sort for you next week, depend upon it. You'll have a safe voyage – and a swift one, if your vessels are as well-found as I'm told they are.'

The master of the *Dunsmore* looked as if he was about to say something more but shrugged without speaking and stood up with the others, who followed the port captain out of the cabin. McCormick laid a hand on Honeyburn's arm.

'If ye'd just wait here a minute, Mr Honeyburn,' he said in a hurried whisper, 'I'd take it as a favour. I'll see 'em down the side and be back in the blink of an eye.'

Left to himself, Honeyburn stood frowning and drumming his fingers on the cabin table. He could hardly have refused, but he wanted to get back to his ship, to the privacy of his cabin where he could consider and plan; the events of this day, none of them happy, seemed to be crowding upon him too fast for cool assessment of their implications. Tomorrow he was to make his first seagoing voyage in command, with a first lieutenant he had not yet seen and whose capability he didn't know; that had been bad enough, but now he was to sail alone, instead of in company and with a senior naval officer to take the responsibility of navigation. And though *Cracker* was basically ready for sea there were dozens of pressing matters to be dealt with, such as the rigging of relieving-tackles and shot-netting for the long six-pounder in its new position after. He suspected that what *Crane*'s captain wanted was an audience for a disquisition on war strategy in the Peninsula.

'Now, Mr Honeyburn,' said McCormick, beginning to talk even before he came in through the cabin door, 'I've marked you down as a man of sense and I'd like your honest opinion.' He reached up to take a long roll of paper from a shelf. 'I've a map here to show the latest disposition of our forces in the Peninsula –'

Honeyburn's heart sank.

3

McCormick's map was in fact the chart of the south-eastern corner of the Bay of Biscay, but it showed a considerable width of the Spanish coast at the bottom and a greater width of the French coast running up its right-hand side. The whole of the Spanish land area, Honeyburn saw as the chart was unrolled on the table, was filled with markings in ink, blocked-in oblongs with arrows sprouting from them, numbers, and scribbled notes. They reached from Santander, which for a while had been Wellington's supply-port before the battle of Vitoria, right to the corner where San Sebastian marked the present limit of the British advance.

''Tis not with the soldiers I'm concerned just now,' McCormick said as he weighted down the ends of the chart with a pair of pistols he had taken from a drawer, 'but with the sea – though sure the sea's the concern as much of the Army as the Navy this minute. For a start, now, consider this.' He planted a forefinger on the chart. 'San Sebastian. The key fortress as Page told us, though he'd have been as cross as briars if I'd told him the same. Here's the French frontier ten miles beyond it. Arthur Wellesley's got ten miles to go before he crosses the Bidassoa into France – but he must take San Sebastian before he can do it. Once he's in France the end's in sight, victory after twenty years of bloody war. D'ye realize that, Honeyburn?'

Honeyburn had not in fact given much thought to the matter, but McCormick's wildly glittering eye was compelling.

'Yes, indeed,' he said.

'And without the troops and the ammunition that comes to him by sea he'd never do it,' McCormick went on. 'Aye, and the food too, for what he'd be getting from the land of Spain wouldn't compare with the seven loaves and a few small fishes. So the fate of the world, ye may say, hangs on a line, and that line the course our convoys steer to the Spanish supply ports, the course your gun-brig will be following tomorrow and meself with an important convoy a week after.' He gave a bark of a laugh. 'To my mind I'm stating the obvious. Does it seem so to you?'

Allowing for the Irishman's high-falutin', thought Honeyburn, what he said was reasonably true.

'It appears plain enough,' he said cautiously.

''Tis as plain as the nose on your face. And if it's that plain to you and me, it's ten times plainer to the French who see their country like to be invaded within days if San Sebastian falls. Why haven't they struck a mighty blow at the convoy line, the British army's lifeline?'

'Why, because our blockade –'

'Just so – precisely. Because every vessel of force they have is bottled-up in their northern ports –' he jabbed his finger at the top of the map – 'with our ships holding 'em fast. And down here south of Cap Ferret what do we find?'

The finger travelled down the straight French coastline on the chart to the Spanish frontier at the corner. 'A hundred miles of coast unguarded, ignored because there are no ports or harbours.'

'There's Bayonne,' remarked Honeyburn, peering at the chart; he felt that he ought to display some interest.

McCormick cocked an eye at him. 'Ah, Bayonne. Five miles inland up a river so silted-up you'd never get your gun-brig in over the bar. Yet there are roads to Bayonne, for wagons and the like.'

He paused as if expecting some comment, but Honeyburn, who was wondering how soon he could decently take his leave, had nothing to say.

'If ye walked north from Bayonne,' McCormick said, 'ye'd have to fly, for there's naught but marsh and lagoons – the Great Bog's nothing to it. The folk that live there get about on stilts, like the sham giant at Drogheda fair. I've a man from Bordeaux in *Crane*, royalist French and rated bosun's mate, and he knows that country well. The Landes, they call it. And d'ye know who governs it? The man Boney pulled out of Spain in disgrace after his failure at Torres Vedras, the ablest of his marshals – Masséna, no less!'

He swung away from the table, swung back again, and confronted his audience with his cheeks puffed out and one eye closed.

'I'm Masséna,' he announced. 'Month after month I've seen the Emperor's armies pushed back towards my country's frontier. Month after month I've seen the enemy's supply-line, the convoys, sailing to and fro and creeping nearer and nearer to my shores as Wellington advances. Would I sit on my arse doing nothing?'

Taking this to be a rhetorical question, Honeyburn was silent. But he was becoming interested despite himself. McCormick flung himself at the chart again.

'See here. This red line's the course laid down by their Lordships for the convoys to this new port of Orio – ye'll know that yourself. It passes within eight leagues of the

French coast. No reefs, no banks, so maybe ye've never looked at the soundings here. Take a look at 'em now.'

Honeyburn peered at the groups of tiny figures where McCormick's finger pointed; then he grunted and peered more closely.

'There's a deep here,' he remarked. 'It appears to run from fifty miles out to right inshore. That's curious. Here's twenty fathoms almost on the shore line, close to a landmark – a church tower, I fancy, though no town is marked.'

'If they had charts five hundred years ago,' said McCormick, 'they'd have marked a town there – and a port. That deep was carved by the Adour river before it changed its course to crawl out past Bayonne, as I have it from my Frenchman, and the mouth of it was a thriving port. There's a bit of an old harbour there still, though the place is no more than a fishing-village. Cap Breton, they call it.' He fixed a glittering eye on Honeyburn. 'And if I was Masséna it's Cap Breton I'd choose for launching my blow at Wellington's lifeline.'

His enthusiasm was infectious. Honeyburn found himself considering the thing seriously.

'If you mean he would build ships there and arm them,' he said after a moment, 'I fear I see no possibility, Mr McCormick. With the inland countryside as you describe it, scarcely inhabited, marshland, no timber, no roads –'

'There's bound to be a track of sorts connecting Cap Breton with Bayonne, and Bayonne a mere dozen miles away. But I'll not hazard a guess how Masséna will do it – it could be fireships, gunboats, infernal machines – I only say it's million to one he'll try something. And mark this, Honeyburn. Next week's convoy is of the first importance, as you've agreed, and if the French got wind of it they'd make a target of it.'

'It's unlikely they'd hear of it, surely.'

'Unlikely, is it? Bless you, they've spies, same as we have.'

Honeyburn scratched his chin, frowning. 'It might be

worthwhile submitting your idea to the naval authorities, Mr McCormick. You have, however, no proof to offer.'

'Not as much proof as would hang a cat.' McCormick spread his hands wide. 'And haven't I written a screed yards long to the Secretary of the Admiralty with never so much as an acknowledgement? And pestered Page with it, who's a fool?'

He reached across to pick up the pistols and the chart, released, rolled itself up with a rustle and a click. McCormick spoke without looking round, apparently addressing the pistols he was holding.

'Proof, now. Here's a neat fast gun-brig sailing for Orio tomorrow and never a vessel with her but herself. Nigh on an independent cruise.' He spun round, his brilliant eyes boring into Honeyburn's. 'D'ye know what I'd do in your place, Honeyburn? I'd bear away eastward south of Cap Ferret – just a point, no more – and I'd take a look, a close look, at Cap Breton. And if that wasn't enough to tell me anything, I'd have a boat put me ashore by night –'

'Good gracious!' Honeyburn was genuinely shocked. 'You must be –' he remembered McCormick's nickname and stopped himself. 'You heard *Cracker*'s orders, Mr McCormick. It's not an independent cruise nor anything like one. She's to carry dispatches, and urgent dispatches, to Orio and I'm expected to bring her there by the twenty-first. Such a – such an escapade as you suggest is quite out of the question.'

'Ye won't do it, then?'

'Certainly not, sir!'

'It might be the salvation of the convoy. It might prove to be a big feather in your –'

'Mr McCormick, I will not go beyond my orders. And I'm surprised,' Honeyburn added somewhat pompously, 'that you should suggest such a thing.' He took his hat from the chair where he had placed it. 'If you'll permit me I'll return to my ship.'

McCormick's face darkened. 'Ah, ye're too long in the

tooth to take chances,' he growled. 'Fitton would have done it. – I beg pardon, Mr Honeyburn,' he added instantly, forcing a smile. 'If ye won't, ye won't, and there's an end to it. A drink, now, before ye go. I've some of the genuine stuff out of Oporto –'

Honeyburn, softening his manner, declined briefly but politely. McCormick saw him to the rail.

'One last word,' he said as Honeyburn swung over onto the ladder. 'They can call me mad if they like, but when *Crane* comes off Cap Breton next week she'll have lookouts at both mastheads. If I catch the hint of a glint of trouble round goes the convoy and away to westward with every stitch set.'

Honeyburn got down to the sternsheets of his waiting boat and was pulled back to *Cracker*. Evening sunlight winked in cheerful reflection from the now waveless harbour waters and gilded the masts and spars of the gun-brig, but he found no pleasure in it. He felt weary – it had been a long day – and dissatisfied with himself. He had been perfectly correct in refusing to consider McCormick's crazy suggestion; yet it was the second time in twenty-four hours (his flight from Cecilia Tuftoe had been the first) that he had shied away from a venture. He was getting old, 'long in the tooth' in McCormick's phrase.

When he got on board there was the solitary 6-pounder aft to remind him of the loss of his cherished bow-chasers. A wordy and technical discussion with the boatswain and the carpenter, the siting of ringbolts and selection of cordage for the new stern-chaser's relieving-tackles, brought him no comfort. Nor did the cold beef and fresh-baked bread that Shorty Band brought to his cabin at eight bells of the second dogwatch. And the first hour of the first watch passed without any sign of his new lieutenant; Mr Fitzjames, told not to come aboard before the first watch, was evidently in no hurry to report. At four bells there was still no Mr Fitzjames. Honeyburn took a turn on deck in the fast-falling twilight, found Sholto and informed him of *Cracker*'s new orders, reminded him that Lieutenant Fitzjames was to be expected, and returned to his cabin. He was very tired and wanted to turn in, but it would be discourteous (he told himself resentfully) to do so before Fitzjames arrived.

Challenge and reply, cheerful shouts and someone singing, signalized the return of the starboard watch from their run ashore. A minute later the boatswain knocked and entered, to report all liberty-men aboard and no trouble.

'And Gomez, sir, he's asked if he can see you,' Sholto added. 'Says there's something he wants to report.'

'Send Gomez in, Mr Sholto, if you please.'

Michael Fitton had thought well enough of Gomez to rate him leading seaman. He had been born in Wapping of Spanish parents, his father, from Bilbao, having settled there. He ducked into the cabin now and knuckled his forehead respectfully, swaying a little on his feet.

'Well, Gomez, what is it?'

Gomez had taken plenty of drink but he had it well in control. His deep voice was only a trifle slurred.

''Twas like this, sir. Some on us was in Pokey's 'Ole, what's a tavern in the lower town, and I see a man as sailed with me pa when 'e 'ad the smuggling schooner – kicked 'im out, did me pa, when 'e found this Garcia was agin the British and for the French. 'E didn't see me at first –'

Gomez had watched the man, saw him talking with men from the crews of the transports, heard them tell him details of the convoys and its new sailing date.

'Which same's been put forward to the eighteenth o' this month,' Gomez added.

'They knew that?' said Honeyburn blankly.

'Aye, sir, all on 'em knew it.'

Aware of Garcia's French leanings, Gomez had started up, intending to grab and question him, but the man had been out of the door before he could lay a hand on him, to vanish in the dark maze of Portsmouth alleys.

'Which I reckoned I did ought to report it to you, sir,' he ended.

'Quite right. Very well, Gomez.'

When the man had gone Honeyburn considered the report, frowning. It was probably impossible to keep that sailing-date secret and Garcia's task had been an easy one. If the man was a spy in French pay, whom would he report to? He could get the information to France, of course – there was still a lot of cross-Channel smuggling – but what could the French do about it? Unless, of course, there was anything in McCormick's Cap Breton fairy-tale, which Honeyburn thought most improbable. The sound of four bells being struck on deck overhead sent the matter out of his mind. Fitzjames was two hours overdue. Perhaps he wasn't coming. Perhaps his unwanted transfer had impelled him to skip, to take himself out of the Service.

Honeyburn was inexpressibly weary. Naval courtesy, he decided, had been sufficiently exercised. He stripped off coat and breeches and rolled into his cot.

He woke hazily aware of sounds in the adjacent cabin and was roused to fuller consciousness by a knock on the door and Sholto's voice.

'Sir! By'r leave, Mr Fitzjames is aboard.'

Honeyburn summoned his wits. 'A moment – I'll get dressed.'

There was a slight pause before the boatswain answered. 'Better leave it till morning, sir. We've put him in his cot. Dead drunk, he is.'

Honeyburn groaned. It needed only this. He lay down again and pulled the blanket over his head.

II

Royal By-blow

1

Honeyburn woke from a dream in which a composite of the Emperor Napoleon and McCormick of the *Crane* was directing the launching of some indeterminate kind of infernal machine for the destruction of the convoy. There was a good deal of accompanying noise – shouts and answers, a hollow rasping sound – and as full consciousness returned he realised that it was the morning swabbing of the deck that had awakened him. This, he remembered, was his last morning in port for a while, with no necessity for hurrying on deck to apprise himself of the conditions of wind and sea and what sail the gun-brig was carrying. He lay for some minutes luxuriating in idleness and contemplating the fading substance of his dream.

There was reason enough behind McCormick's basic assumption, he reflected; the French must have seen that an effective blow at Wellington's supply-line could turn the tide of war against him and perhaps save France from invasion. The rest was nonsense, for they were powerless to strike such a blow. They would need ships of force, ships capable of cruising on the convoy route for days on end until their chance came, and the whole of their naval strength was securely held in the ports and harbours north of the Landes coast. It was only two months since Wellington had crossed the Ebro to show at Salamanca and Vitoria that his threat to chase the French armies over the

Pyrenees into their own country was no empty one; to imagine that in that short time the enemy could have built ships somewhere in the desolate region behind the hundred miles of sand-dunes on their Biscay coast, and were prepared to launch them from a decayed mediaeval harbour – well, it justified McCormick's nickname. He dismissed the matter from his thoughts and considered the more immediate problem of his crew shortage. Captain Page was probably right when he assured the merchant captains that there was now no likelihood of enemy attack in the Bay, but if *Cracker* did happen to encounter a prowling *chasse-marée* or a privateer of *Lexington*'s force she was in no very good shape for a fight. He had the bare minimum of hands to provide gun-crews for one broadside – six of his twelve 18-pounder carronades – and that left no one to man the long 6-pounder that had now been sited on his little quarterdeck, in his opinion the most valuable gun in the ship since it possessed twice the effective range of the carronades. And the thought of the long six reminded him that the removal of two heavy guns from for'ard and the installation of one of them aft meant a palpable alteration in *Cracker*'s trim. He would have to confer with Sholto, probably have the water-casks shifted –

At this point his thoughts brought themselves up with a round turn. He knew that these various topics had presented themselves as a means of shying-away from the more urgent – and more unpleasant – problem of how he was to deal with Lieutenant Fitzjames.

Honeyburn was by nature a kindly man and of a sensibility that was at times inconvenient. His ten years in the Royal Navy had taught him the necessity of cultivating the fierce aspect, the autocratic voice and bearing, that alone could deal efficiently with laggards and offenders, though he could never bring himself to employ the customary naval oaths. But he had spent fifteen years as a schoolmaster, and he was well aware of the wholly disproportionate effect of the small tragedies of youth, the burning disappointments, the deep-thrusting hopeless passions; effects forgotten or laughed-at in later life but seeming at the time as momentous as the end of the world. His resolution last night before dropping off to sleep had been that tomorrow he would come the outraged senior officer over Mr Fitzjames, give him the tongue-lashing he deserved for failing to report and coming on board drunk. But this morning his old sympathies with the young asserted themselves. Fitzjames must be eighteen or nineteen, he reflected as he rolled out of his hanging cot; little more than a boy. Made lieutenant three weeks ago and no doubt proud of his new rank. Proud of his ship too, probably (Honeyburn pulled on his trousers) for *Centaur* was a crack 74, though Decies was reputed to be a flogging captain. He's suddenly transferred willy-nilly to a humble gun-brig – Etheridge would have told him why – commanded by an ex-schoolmaster who's expected to teach him Lower-Form Latin and Greek. It was no great wonder that the lad had tried to drown resentment and frustration in drink.

Honeyburn donned his uniform coat and cocked hat and went up on deck. A cool morning for the time of year, the sun not yet up above the houses of the port, the few fleecy clouds in the pale blue overhead coming across from eastward – a fair wind, if it held, for that afternoon's sailing. The hands of the swabbing-and-scouring party had just finished flogging the decks dry and were up for'ard hanging their cloths on a line rigged between the foremast shrouds, and the boatswain, his thickset figure neatly clad as usual in dark-blue round coat and clean white breeches, was coming aft along the deck.

'Morning, sir,' said Sholto.

'Good morning, Mr Sholto. I'd like a word with you concerning her trim. With the bow-chasers gone –' Honeyburn stopped suddenly. 'We'll go into it later, if you please. Pray oblige me by going for'ard for a moment.'

'Aye aye, sir.'

Sholto hid a grin as he turned away. Honeyburn took a

pace towards the figure he had seen slouching towards him from the after-cabins and halted, his expression amiable but unsmiling.

'Mr Fitzjames?'

'George Fitzjames.' It was a sullen mumble. 'Reporting for duty.'

He was a little below Honeyburn's height, dark-haired and black-browed, well enough looking if it hadn't been for the sulky droop of the stubborn mouth and the pallid cheeks and red-rimmed eyes. His blue coat was plainly new but sadly creased and crumpled, as were his wine-stained white trousers, and the cocked hat he had touched with a perfunctory forefinger as he spoke was put on askew.

'Welcome aboard, Mr Fitzjames,' Honeyburn said formally. 'We'll walk the quarterdeck, if you please.' Turning, he caught the contemptuous curl of the lips. 'There is of course no true quarterdeck in a flush-decked brig as in a seventy-four,' he added, 'but thus we denominate these three fathoms for'ard of the six-pounder.'

Fitzjames said nothing. His bearing as he paced up and down the prescribed space beside Honeyburn was that of a reluctant small boy compelled by his nurse to walk sedately.

'You'll permit me, I hope,' Honeyburn said pleasantly, 'to remind you of two things. The first is that although we are nominally of the same rank – I, however, being the senior lieutenant by virtue of my commission bearing a date earlier than yours – you are now in the position of first lieutenant in a vessel of which I am the captain. It's usual, I believe, for a first lieutenant to use the word 'sir' when addressing his captain. You'll remember that, of course, in future.'

He waited, and the due response came in a mumble: 'Aye aye, sir' – but there was a marked pause before the *sir* which was certainly intended to annoy. It was many years since Honeyburn had been as drunk as Fitzjames was last night but he could remember the splitting headache and the resultant animosity towards the world in general that followed such indulgences and ignored the rudeness.

'The second matter,' he went on evenly, 'is this. It's possible, though I doubt it, that Captain Decies allows his officers to come on board *Centaur* drunk. Whether or not, it's not the custom in *Cracker*. You'll oblige me, Mr Fitzjames, by not doing it again.'

'Aye aye, sir.' It was a growl between clenched teeth this time.

'We are under orders to sail,' Honeyburn continued without change of tone as they turned, 'and I anticipate it will be shortly after noon. Dispatches are being sent on board which we are to carry to Orio. Do you know Orio?'

'No,' said Fitzjames. 'Sir.'

'A small port – roadstead but no harbour – four leagues east of Bilbao. You and I will stand watch-and-watch while we're at sea. When we cast-off moorings you'll take the foredeck. In action – though we're not very like to see any – you'll be in charge of the for'ard guns. I am necessarily brief since there are matters to be attended to before we sail. Pray ask if there is anything you wish to know.'

'There's one question, sir.'

Fitzjames was not mumbling now, and for the first time, as he halted and turned to face his senior, there was some trace of expression on his pale features, a gleam that was rather anxiety than hostility in the grey eyes. The sun had just topped the eastward rooftops and in its clear light he looked younger than his nineteen years.

'That fellow Etheridge came aboard here yesterday,' he said awkwardly.

'Yes.' Since Fitzjames seemed to have some difficulty in continuing Honeyburn helped him out. 'Mr Etheridge appeared to expect me to extend my duties as captain to include those of a tutor. I must tell you in all honesty, Mr Fitzjames, that I can give little time if any –'

'It's not that. I suppose he told you of my birth?'

'He did.' Honeyburn's face and voice were as expressionless as he could make them.

Fitzjames hesitated and then spoke in a rush. 'Sir – does

anyone of this ship's company know of it besides yourself?'

'Not to my knowledge, and I would consider it unlikely. I hope I needn't add that neither they nor anyone else will ever hear of it through me, Mr Fitzjames.'

As he was speaking the boatswain, who had been hovering uncertainly a few paces away, made up his mind and stepped nearer.

'By'r leave, sir – hands to breakfast?'

Honeyburn took his watch from his fob and glanced at it. 'Make it so, Mr Sholto, if you please.'

Sholto turned for'ard and put his silver call to his lips. The piercing bubbling note rose and fell as he departed and Fitzjames winced and put a hand involuntarily to his head.

'You'll take breakfast with me in my cabin, Mr Fitzjames?' said Honeyburn; over bowls of Hezekiah Band's excellent burgoo, he was thinking, the ice of this curious encounter might be still further broken.

But the sullen mask was back again and the muttered reply was ungracious.

'Can't eat breakfast – beg to be excused, sir.'

'Very well.' Honeyburn was brief. 'On deck at six bells, if you please.'

He turned and went down to his cabin without waiting for the *aye aye, sir* which Fitzjames might or might not say. Band was there within the minute with the breakfast tray.

'Good mornin', sir, there's cream with the cawfee, got it orf of a bumboat but I've 'ad a taste an' it's fresh. Them wet duds o' yourn, sir, I've got 'em out a-hairin' an' they'll be fit to wear afore eight bells.'

'Thank you, Band. Take a cup of coffee to Mr Fitzjames's cabin – black, with no cream or sugar.'

'Aye, aye, sir.'

There was the dawn of a grin on Band's round face and he seemed about to risk a wink; but grin and wink perished unfulfilled beneath his captain's cold stare. Left to himself, Honeyburn applied himself to coffee and burgoo. He was fond of oatmeal and Band had the knack of making it without those unappetising lumps, but his thoughts were elsewhere and he frowned as he ate. It was plain that he was going to have trouble with Fitzjames. The lad not only fiercely disliked his appointment to *Cracker* but he was also stubbornly determined that his dislike should be apparent to everyone, including his new commanding officer.

He was not, Honeyburn was convinced, naturally slovenly and ill-mannered; it was an attitude he had resolved, in the pig-headed manner of youth, to adopt and maintain by way of showing his self-sufficiency. His bastardy, of course, had a part in this. Honeyburn had known men who would have boasted of having royal blood in their veins, whether it was put there on the wrong side of the blanket or not. Evidently young Fitzjames was not of this sort. He was ashamed of being a bastard, carried a chip on his shoulder; probably – it was common in such cases – hated the man, the descendant of Stuarts and Hanoverian princelings, who had fathered him.

Well – Honeyburn finished his coffee, which was having its roborant effect – a day or two at sea might put an end to the youngster's attitudinising and in the meantime he would ignore it as far as he could. If Fitzjames was fool enough to let it affect his duty, of course, it was another matter and he would have to discipline him according to the usage of the Service. He very much hoped that wouldn't happen. It could mean the ruin of Fitzjames's naval career; and he found something likeable about Fitzjames despite his brutish behaviour.

When he came on deck Portsmouth Harbour was fully alive, wherries and cutters scudding to and fro on the lively breeze, a clatter of hammers from the dockyard, a multitudinous but muted din of shouts, chanties, distant challenges. The wind was still steady in the east. Fitzjames was already on deck, standing by the rail and gazing across at the moored 74's as an exile might gaze at the country he was about to leave for ever.

'Mr Fitzjames! I'll introduce our warrant-officers and

we'll make a quick tour of the ship, if you please.'

Fitzjames had spun round with a boy's alertness on hearing his name. Obviously recollecting himself, he shambled across the deck and they walked for'ard together. The boatswain had a party at work rousing-out the spare cable on the foredeck. Being hatless, he knuckled his forehead as Honeyburn performed the brief formal introduction. There was no sign on his broad weatherbeaten face that he remembered hauling his new first lieutenant inboard and carrying him to his cabin with Peters's assistance, and it was to presumed that Mr Fitzjames had no recollection of it at all. A finger to his hat and an inarticulate grunt was all Fitzjames vouchsafed in reply to Sholto's 'Welcome aboard, sir,' and it was the same with Mr Grattan, discovered scouring pots in his galley. The carpenter, whom they found sharpening a chisel in the tiny cubbyhole he had contrived for himself between his cabin and the mess-deck, had as usual more to say than the others.

"Appy to 'ave you with us, sir,' said Mr Trapp, visibly unlimbering his bony jaw. 'You'll find 'er a good sea-boat, a good sea-boat, I say, as'll stay in 'er own length, or nigh enough, when rightly 'andled, and fast on a wind as the cap'n 'ere will tell you –'

'Yes indeed, Mr Trapp.'

Honeyburn's tone was intended to cut him short but Mr Trapp was not to be so quickly checked.

'Yes, sir – though 'er best point o' sailing, as we know, is with the wind just a trifle, just a trifle, I say, abaft the beam. And furthermore to that, sir, on the same tack, you might say, this heasterly what's a fine fair wind for 'er, it'll 'old, sir, for a day or two and mebbe more.' He paused, his watery blue eyes challenging them to contest it, and then added, 'That's *my* prognostification.'

'Mr Trapp is a better weather-prophet than most barometers, Mr Fitzjames,' said Honeyburn. 'He's sailed these waters, and for that matter the seven seas, all his life.'

'Sixty-five year, man and boy,' nodded the carpenter.

'Aye, man and boy, first shipping in the old *R'yal Oak* at the Nore what carried sixty great guns –'

'Thank you, Mr Trapp,' Honeyburn said firmly, and they walked on.

He had thought he detected a quiver of his companion's lip when Mr Trapp pronounced his six-syllable word but otherwise Fitzjames's expression had not varied its stony sullenness. And the twitching lip could have been the ghost of a scornful smile. As they proceeded with their tour of the ship – mess-deck, sail locker, cable locker, magazine, store-hold – Honeyburn found his brief expositions growing briefer still because of the lack of response. Fitzjames, when he couldn't avoid answering without giving plain offence, confined himself to 'yes, sir' and 'no, sir'.

It was the same when they rejoined the boatswain to discuss the amendment to *Cracker*'s trim. Fitzjames silently declined to be drawn into the discussion though he was given plenty of opportunity, restricting himself to monosyllabic agreement when he had to speak. His manner stopped just short of rudeness, and Honeyburn sensed rather than discerned from look or tone of voice the young man's growing contempt for his new ship and her ways. Doubtless Decies of the *Centaur* wouldn't have brooked Mr Trapp's garrulity or given way to the boatswain's forcible argument that all the water-casks, not half of them, would have to be shifted from number one to number two hold to compensate for the alteration in her armament; and Honeyburn himself had probably lost more than he had gained in the article of respect by his comparative tolerance. He was not going to change his present course, however, unless and until Fitzjames displayed similar slackness in his duties as first lieutenant.

'Very well, Mr Sholto,' he said, terminating the conference. 'We'll shift every cask. Detail a party and muster them on the foredeck. Then I'll thank you to make a round of all running rigging and see that all's clear for casting off. Mr Fitzjames, take charge of the working-party. Stow the water-casks even numbers port and starboard, have them properly lashed down and test the lashings yourself.'

He spoke incisively and Fitzjames's 'aye aye, sir' held a hint of surprise. Honeyburn hadn't waited for it, however, but had turned and stalked away aft. As he went below to his cabin he was feeling markedly dissatisfied with himself. All he seemed to have done by his policy of restraint and tolerance was to give Fitzjames the impression that his new commander was fussy, ineffective, and inclined to be pompous. Well, the Articles of War could be invoked when an officer was lacking in zeal or slack in performance of his duty; the next day or two would decide whether or not his first lieutenant was going to push his childish sulkiness too far.

He opened the chart locker and rummaged among the rolled cylinders of stiff paper for the charts of the western Channel and its approaches. In a gun-brig there was no sailing-master, the officer in command being expected to do his own navigation, and though he was familiar enough with all the bearings and departures – *Cracker* had made the voyage to northern Spain five times – he wanted to refresh his memory. He was an adequate navigator on paper but less certain in assessing such external influences as local currents and the set of the tides.

The first chart that came to hand was a captured French one that had been presented to Michael Fitton by his friend Gardiner of the frigate *Princess Charlotte*, who was now on the Spanish coast. It was a recent edition, since it showed the depths in metres, the new French units. Honeyburn half-unrolled it for a quick glance. It was the chart of the Biscay coast of France south of Arcachon, with rather more detail inland from the coast than was shown on the Admiralty chart, and his eye fell at once on the name Cap Breton. So the information McCormick had got from his bosun's mate had some foundation in fact, though apart from the name and the cross that signified a church there was not much else. A very small inlet that could indicate a harbour was marked – if shown correctly to scale it must be very small indeed – and he noted a narrow lake or lagoon just north of the inlet and running parallel to the coast not a mile west of it. Could this lagoon, nearly three miles long according to the French chart, lend any support to McCormick's theories? He pondered frowning for some moments and decided that it couldn't. It remained impossible that in such a place, islanded between wide marshes and the sea, the French could have constructed a vessel or vessels of sufficient size to threaten the British convoys.

He laid the chart aside and found the one that showed the Island and its flanking seaways. His study of this was accompanied by the hollow thuds and rumblings of the cask-shifting; and at one point he heard Fitzjames's voice raised in the longest utterance he had so far heard from that laconic youth. It was a powerful voice, and Fitzjames was using it as he had no doubt learned from *Centaur*'s lieutenants. *Handsomely, God damn your eyes ... haul taut, I said, you poxed son of a bitch* ... followed by a couple of filthier epithets. Honeyburn grimaced and then shrugged; he himself was opposed to strong language, particularly when it was used to a man who couldn't answer back, but he knew this made him an eccentric. A first lieutenant was expected to have a good swearing vocabulary – and at least it was clear that Fitzjames was taking his work seriously. All the same, he would have to make him understand that foul language was not customary in *Cracker*.

He returned to his study of the charts. The noise of the cask-stowing ceased. Six bells sounded overhead. The noonday sun's heat on the deck above him was producing an oven-like atmosphere in the little cabin and he was stowing the charts preparatory to going on deck when Sholto put his head in through the open door.

'Boat alongside, sir – package for you from the port captain.'

Cauthery, duty lieutenant, was stepping over the rail as Honeyburn came on deck. They exchanged salutes and

Cauthery handed over the two packets he carried, one covered in oiled canvas with a bar of lead sewn into its covering and the other a letter with the Admiralty seal.

'Captain Page's compliments and you may sail immediately,' said Cauthery. 'Lucky devil!' he added. 'Fair wind at this end and fair senoritas at t'other.'

Honeyburn thanked him, saw him down the side, and cast a quick glance all round. Slack water; at the moment a clear run to the harbour entrance; lying as she did, the gun-brig must cast-off her bow cable first so that the breeze on her starboard bow would swing her gently ready to take the wind. On her deck, he saw, preparations for casting-off were already in hand – there was not a man on board who didn't know by this time that *Cracker* was to sail as soon as her orders came aboard. Sholto had the topmen standing by, on the topsail yards the sails were brailed-up, and Fitzjames was moving, albeit sluggishly, to his station right for'ard. He broke the seal of the letter: sail forthwith for Orio – dispatches to be delivered by you in person to the captain of that port – an indecipherable signature with 'Secretary to the Admiralty' in more legible handwriting beneath it. He drew a deep breath and let it out in a shout.

'Hands to unmoor ship! Mr Fitzjames! Cast off, if you please.'

There was no hitch. Fitzjames's shout of 'All gone for'ard!' heralded the start of the swing as *Cracker*'s bows angled away from the line of moored ships, the topmen raced up the shrouds and cast off the brailings, standing poised on the footropes and holding the canvas; the yo-hoing party aft brought the stern cable aboard.

'Let fall – sheets, sheet home – belay.' The billowing topsails drew taut and the gun-brig, leaning slightly to the wind on her beam, began to draw away from her place. 'Full and bye, Erikson,' said Honeyburn to the man at the wheel.

'*Cracker* ahoy!'

They were passing a long pistol-shot from *Crane* and there was McCormick at the rail, his long black hair blowing wildly in the breeze.

'Mr Honeyburn, remember what I told ye!' he yelled. 'Take a look if ye can, and the saints go with ye!'

Honeyburn raised a hand by way of acknowledgement and then they were past, steering for the harbour mouth.

2

His Majesty's Ship *Cracker* was not, strictly speaking, a ship at all, despite the facts that her people were a ship's company and her log a Ship's Log. She was a brig, as her two masts with their square sails betokened. But in addition to the four tiers of canvas she could hoist on main and foremast she could wear three jibs on her long bowsprit – more than a third of the ship's whole length – and these with the spanker on its even longer boom aft gave her some measure of a schooner's efficiency on a wind. As she flew down-Channel into the eye of the setting sun she made a picture to delight the eye of any seaman, more graceful (though much smaller) than a frigate because she lacked the frigate's clumsy beakhead and high poop, the bow-wave at her forefoot and her towers of canvas equally tinted red-gold in the declining rays, as much at home in the wide spaces of sea and sky as the gulls that cruised and called above her creaming wake.

It was remarkable weather for the Channel, even in summer. In his five passages westward out of Portsmouth Honeyburn had known nothing like it; on one occasion (though that had been in March) it had taken *Cracker* a week of strenuous beating before she made her landfall off the Lizard. today she had left the Needles astern at two bells of the first dog and brought Portland Bill on the beam before two bells of the second dog. The wind, full and steady from a little south of east, gave her nine, ten, even eleven knots under sail to the topgallants; and the oracular Mr Trapp declared that it showed every sign of continuosity.

Some few of the hands no doubt regretted exchanging the delights of Portsmouth town for the wholly masculine society of a ship at sea, but the majority were tired of the summer stinks and enclosing wharves of the harbour and would have been glad to sail even if it meant a week of beating against gale and rain. With this perfection of sailing weather and the prospect of a fast run, every hand on board was in high spirits. The exhilaration of air and sea and swift motion seemed to have a certain amount of effect on *Cracker*'s first lieutenant; he continued to present a glum and slovenly front and to repel any approach to conversation, but Honeyburn suspected that he did so with difficulty.

There had been two brief exchanges between Fitzjames and the captain after *Cracker* had passed the harbour entrance. The first had been when they were making sail, getting courses and inner jib on her, and Fitzjames, deciding that the men aloft were too slow, had made his opinion known with some particularly filthy oaths uttered at the top of his voice. Honeyburn had called him aft as soon as the sheets were belayed.

'Mr Fitzjames,' he said easily, 'we give to necessity the praise of virtue, or at least Quintillian tells us so. But there is no virtue in using the sort of language I've just heard you use, for it is perfectly unnecessary. Moreover, the hands will not respect you for it.'

'It's the only language they understand,' Fitzjames growled sullenly.

'I don't know who told you that,' Honeyburn said with more asperity, 'but I take leave to doubt it. In any case, you will please to conform to my wishes. I'm well aware that reprimands need to be given sharply and firmly, but in future you'll oblige me by not giving them in language redolent of the cesspool behind a pothouse.'

If Fitzjames appreciated this picturesque phrase he gave no sign of it. He muttered 'Aye aye, sir' between his teeth and turned to slouch away.

The second occasion was ten minutes later, when Honeyburn had ordered topgallants on fore and main. This time there was some excuse for reprimands, for Nolan and Driscoll, *Cracker*'s two Irishmen, had collided as they ran out on the main topgallant yard and had paused to exchange blows. Fitzjames's voice – it was deep for a young man and he could sound savage when he liked – rang out instantly in a continuous volley of words that had immediate effect; more by its tone than by its content, Honeyburn thought. He had a modest fluency in the French language himself, but much of Fitzjames's utterance, barring *merde* and one or two similar expressions, was beyond his vocabulary. It was a sort of schoolboy impertinence, of course, but he had to hide a smile when the young man came aft at his summons.

'You have a repertory of French imprecations, it seems, Mr Fitzjames.'

'You don't object, sir, I trust?'

Honeyburn ignored the sarcastic tone. 'No-o-o. It appeared to impress Driscoll and Nolan, and if it satisfies your sense of what is proper in the circumstances, well and good. But I'd like to ask, if I may, where you acquired such a command of the language.'

'There was a Frenchman, a vicomte, in the gunroom aboard *Centaur*,' Fitzjames replied shortly.

'And you profited by his acquaintance,' Honeyburn nodded. 'Very well, Mr Fitzjames. Carry on – or *continuez*, if you prefer it.'

For a fleeting instant their eyes met and Honeyburn thought he saw in Fitzjames's a twinkle of amusement. But the deliberate slouch was there still when he turned – somewhat abruptly, as though unwilling to expose himself to further pleasantries – and went for'ard.

And *Cracker* sped on across blue-ridged waves thinly crested with white, flying for hours on end with no need for sheet or halliard to be touched or sail handed. It was a populous sea she crossed, sails far and near especially to starboard where the English coast lay just below the horizon. They overhauled and spoke a brigantine out of Weymouth, bound by her own account for Falmouth but more probably (Honeyburn thought) for Roscoff in Brittany on the smuggling trade. That probability reminded him of the spy, if spy he was, that Gomez had tried to catch in the Portsmouth tavern. In some craft like the brigantine the man's news concerning the convoy sailing-date could reach France: and Roscoff, though a long way to northward, was not unhandy to the Biscay coast – and much handier to the French naval bases at Brest and Rochefort. But what could they do about it, if the news ever reached them? Nothing, permanently imprisoned in their ports as they were by the British blockade. There was indeed, he reflected, visualising the map of France, a long, long gap between the blockading squadrons and the other concentration of British ships to southward, the transports and supply-vessels and escorts plying to and fro along the north coast of Spain. Where the route of the convoys crossed that gap would be the place for the enemy to strike with little or no likelihood of opposition from British warships of any force. That was McCormick's theory; but he was Mad McCormick after all, and Honeyburn had decided already that his premises were shaky and his conclusion unsound.

At sunset *Cracker* was well out across the bight of Lyme Bay, with the Devon coast 25 miles to northward, and while there was still light enough to see by Honeyburn ordered her topgallants to be taken in. He was irritably aware of Fitzjames's raised eyebrows and curl of the lip but he took no overt notice. It was a hackneyed jibe of the Royal Navy that timorous merchant captains always reduced sail at night, though in a seaway as busy as the western Channel it was a sensible enough precaution; but Honeyburn's chief reason for reducing his speed was that the sun would not rise until twenty minutes after the end of the middle watch. He was determined to take a good departure when the time came for *Cracker* to alter course and head south-west to clear Ushant, and that time would come when he made his landfall off the Start, a landfall for which the light of day would be needed. He saw no reason to explain that to Fitzjames. A naval captain did not make excuses for his decisions to a first lieutenant.

Honeyburn, like others of his temperament, found it easier to bear with major afflictions than with smaller ones, and the succession of small absurd annoyances Fitzjames saw fit to inflict on him was beginning to wear out his patience. It was not yet exhausted, however, and at the changing of the watch he made another attempt at sociability. Keeping watch-on, watch-off as they were, his first lieutenant would have the deck for the first watch, until midnight. For all Fitzjames's ridiculous behaviour Honeyburn had seen nothing to suggest that he was not capable of keeping a watch, and there would be a warrant officer to support him; Mr Trapp and Mr Sholto kept watch-and-watch on deck at sea (the cook being excused this duty) and Sholto, whose habit it was to walk up and down amidships, would be at hand in emergency. At eight bells of the last dog, therefore, he duly handed over.

'Here you have her, Mr Fitzjames,' he said formally. 'Courses and tops'ls, inner and outer jibs. Course sou'-west by west, lookouts at foremast and bows to be relieved at four bells. You find your quarters sufficiently comfortable, I hope?'

'Yes, sir.'

It was too dark to see the young man's face but if it matched his voice it was devoid of expression.

'After the midshipman's berth in a seventy-four, perhaps, the solitude of a private cabin could be almost oppressive. Do you find it so?'

'No, sir.'

Honeyburn tried again. 'For my part, I welcomed it when I was made lieutenant. I'd been by far the oldest midshipman in an eighty-gun ship of the line which carried seven of us – indeed, I recall that the combined ages of the other six in the gunroom totalled precisely twice my own age – so you may conceive my lack of *rapport* with them.'

To this confidence Fitzjames made no reply at all. Honeyburn gave it up.

'Call me if the wind changes, if you please,' he said briefly, and went below.

As he rolled into his hanging cot he reflected glumly on Shakespeare's assertion that crabbed age and youth cannot live together. He was not old, of course – far from it – but to a youth of eighteen he must seem so; Honeyburn could remember that as a lad of Fitzjames's age he had thought of all men who had reached the age of fifty as being practically in their dotage. No doubt the boy saw him as an elderly incompetent, over-cautious and given to stilted utterance. As to Fitzjames's obstinate persistence in the sulks, Honeyburn in his years in charge of adolescent youth had often seen sillier behaviour indulged in for less cause.

However (he told himself angrily, turning over in the cot) it was not incumbent on him to find excuses for Fitzjames, who was wholly and solely at fault. A sound birching judiciously applied, he recalled, had worked wonders with one of those awkward cases at Westminster, but you couldn't birch a King's officer. What was needed was sharp action of another kind – a sea-fight like the duel with *Lexington* in June would shake the nonsense out of Fitzjames. Even a sudden deterioration in the weather, a battle with one of those savage gales (*Cracker* had only just survived one in March) would suffice, he felt sure, to strip away the boy's self-imposed aloofness. He grinned wryly as he pulled the blanket round his shoulders; it was a measure of his concern with this fiddling problem that he should find himself wishing for bad weather.

There was no change in the weather that night. The steady easterly wafted the gun-brig steadily on her course over the long smooth Atlantic rollers coming in past the Scillies. At midnight Honeyburn took over the deck from his laconic first lieutenant, who had nothing to report. He was in no mood to invite a further rebuff by attempting conversation, and Mr Trapp, who also had the middle watch, soon found his captain unresponsive and left him to his solitary pacing of the little quarterdeck. Peters, at the wheel, knew better than to speak before he was spoken to and was silent when – more than once – Honeyburn came to peer at the compass by the glow of the binnacle lamp. The windy stars overhead paled slowly, the clear sky astern showed a lifting light, and from the foremast-head the lookout hailed.

'On deck, there! Land-ho – land broad on the stabb'd bow!'

A good landfall. Honeyburn felt the warm glow of satisfaction that comes to the man whose calculations of course and dead-reckoning have proved themselves perfectly accurate. His yell, as penetrating as the high notes of a trumpet, roused *Cracker* to intense activity. Men raced aloft to let fall the topgallants, the spanker yard rose until its big sail tautened, the helm came slowly over to bring the wind on her port quarter. With the Start dead astern, the gun-brig raced away on the fifty-league run to her next landfall off Ushant.

3

The wind continued to blow steadily from the east, though with some lessening of its strength, all through the second day of *Cracker*'s voyage. At four bells of the first dog-watch the hail from the lookout came, and Honeyburn took his glass to the masthead – an ascent he never really enjoyed – to examine the landfall for himself. The tiny mark notching the blue horizon to port could only be Ushant, Ile d'Ouessant on the French charts, and again his navigation had been faultless. Not that there was overmuch credit in that, he told himself as he stepped sedately down the shrouds; in such weather even a landsman, if he could read a chart and use a compass, could hardly have gone off course. Still, it was satisfactory, an easing of the mind after an uneasy day.

It had been an uneventful day. The swift unvarying flight across the long white-feathered rollers had been diversified only by the gun-brig's routine: the swabbing of the deck, hammocks piped up, breakfast; the regular sequence of clangs on the ship's bell; hands to dinner after noon and the issue of grog; quarters, hammocks piped down, the setting of the watch. They had sighted only two sail on the vast expanse of sunlit blue and those too far away to be spoken. And throughout the day Lieutenant Fitzjames had preserved his attitude of disdainful aloofness and – so far as he could – an uncompromising silence. There was no overt offence that Honeyburn could lay a finger on; he might show no proper alacrity when obeying an order but he was brisk enough in seeing that it was carried out. It was his whole bearing, his attitude of apathy and half-concealed contempt for all about him, that Honeyburn found increasingly exasperating. It was as though Fitzjames flaunted an unspoken defiance: *I'm here against my will and come what may I'll never become one of this ship's company.*

It was this in particular that wrought upon Honeyburn's patience. He himself, landsman though he was by upbringing, had come to love *Cracker* and to take the pride in her which a man takes in the house that is his only home. The contempt and dislike for her that Fitzjames seemed to feel, or at least saw fit to display, was to his mind as insufferable as a guest's open disparagement of his host's possessions. In vain he told himself that he was making too much of a small matter, magnifying pinpricks into a wound. The thing rankled. When he took over the watch at sunrise he was as curt and unsmiling as his first lieutenant, and the dazzling advent of the sun's rim climbing above the sea horizon on the port hand failed to bring its usual lift of spirits.

Hardly had Fitzjames gone below when Mr Trapp came trotting along the deck.

'By'r leave, sir –'

'Well, Mr Trapp?'

Mr Trapp cleared his throat. 'It's my belief, sir, I say it's my belief, as 'ow she ain't changed 'er rate of sailin' by so much as 'arf a knot all night. Ten-and-a-'arf we was loggin' at sundown and I'll take me davy that's what she's loggin' now.' His sharp old eyes regarded his captain much as a spaniel's who hoped to be taken a walk. 'If I might suggest it, sir –'

'Very well, Mr Trapp. Heave the log, if you please.'

It looked as if the carpenter had been waiting for Fitzjames's departure, for at his hoarse call Gomez at once came aft carrying the reel of log-line and the wooden log, with Tubbs at his heels bearing the thirty-second sandglass. Tubbs was the elder of *Cracker*'s two ship's boys, a shock-headed youth of 14. The three went to the lee rail. Tubbs held the reel above his head by the two handles and Mr Trapp took the sandglass and held it to his eye. Gomez threw the log overside and called 'Turn!' Mr Trapp upended the sandglass and peered eagerly at the falling grains like a venerable eagle scrutinizing a toothsome morsel, while the line running out from the reel set Tubb's arms a-quiver and Gomez let it slip smoothly through his fingers.

'Nip!' squeaked the carpenter sharply, and bent to see where Gomez's fingers had nipped and checked the line. 'Ten-and-a-'arf knots, sir, if you please!' he cried triumphantly. 'Just as I said. And still blowin' steady, doo east. If the wind 'olds, if it 'olds, I say, sir, she'll make this run in phenomenable time.'

The boatswain had come aft while he was speaking.

'Morning, sir,' said Sholto, screwing up his eyes against the brilliant sunlight. 'Wind's moderated just a trifle, all the same.'

He tilted his head to stare up considerably at the three tiers of taut white canvas, and Honeyburn grinned inwardly; Sholto could never bear to see *Cracker* doing less than her best.

'Yes, Mr Sholto. And I believe we'll get the royals on her before breakfast is piped.'

'Aye aye, sir!' said Sholto with intense satisfaction, and trotted for'ard bellowing for the topmen.

The log-heaving party had gone – it was Mr Trapp's watch-below – and except for Timmis at the wheel Honeyburn had the after-deck to himself. He began to pace the ten yards of his little quarterdeck, at each turn forward glancing aloft to where the topmen wrestled with the gaskets of the royals. The sails flashed out, flapped, bellied, and were drawn taut; he felt the slight but definite pull, the increased tilt of the deck under his feet, as the gun-brig responded. Spray from her bow-wave leapt above her starboard bow at intervals, glittering like a fountain of diamonds. It was indeed a beautiful morning, though already the haze inseparable from a persistent east wind was beginning to blur the empty horizon, and his spirits rose. His first voyage in command, and conditions so far as perfect as they could be – he could almost forget Fitzjames in gloating over his good fortune.

He busied himself with calculations as he paced. *Cracker* was crossing the long curving bight of the west coast of France which lay some ninety miles away on her port hand; a dangerous coast apart from its human hostility, rock-bound and defended by reefs and shoals, a lee shore more often than not for the inshore squadrons watching over Brest and the naval ports farther south. Honeyburn's dead-reckoning position at sunset yesterday had been thirty leagues west of Quiberon Bay; he must now, he reckoned, be west of Rochefort, and a few leagues nearer to the coast because of its curve and his converging course. That gave him something like 180 sea-miles to cover to Orio. At this rate of sailing – which postulated no change in the force or direction of the wind – *Cracker* would be off Orio before midnight of this present day, the 18th. He would have to shorten sail so as not to come in to Orio, an unknown port and a small one, until the morning light of the 19th; but even so he would make port two days earlier than expected. Mr Trapp's 'phenomenable' was not too strong a word for so expeditious a passage.

Meanwhile, he reminded himself, he had been two full days at sea without exercising the guns. The forenoon watch would be a good time for that.

Four bells of the forenoon watch found *Cracker*'s deck alive with hurrying men running to their stations at the guns of the port broadside. They flung off the canvas spray covers, cast loose the tackles, and stood ready, four men to each of the six 18-pounder carronades, with one other hand and the two ship's boys as ammunition supply. There should have been a man or boy for each gun, to run back and forth from the magazine below decks where Mr Grattan was stationed, but with the gun-brig's crew so depleted there would have been too few hands left to sail the ship in action. Behind the guns stood the two officers in charge of them, Mr Fitzjames for the for'ard guns and Mr Sholto for the remaining three. Fitzjames's posture, as usual slack and slouched, contrived to suggest his utter indifference to the whole proceeding. Honeyburn, eyeing him from his stance on the quarterdeck, repressed a strong impulse to stride for'ard and give his lieutenant a good shaking. He sent a quick glance at each waiting group.

It was eminently satisfactory that he knew every one of them and his capabilities. During *Cracker*'s stay in Portsmouth he had had to mark 'R' against two names in the muster-book, names of men who had run, deserted; and Halling, ship's boy eleven years old, had been taken ashore very ill. His failure to bring his crew up to complement at least meant that he had no pressed men, no gaolbirds, who must be taught everything from the beginning. The men under his eye were all old Crackers, men who had fought those guns in the action with *Lexington*. They could be trusted not to leave the sponge-and-rammer in the muzzle or get in the way of the recoil; though as this was merely drill there would be no recoil except the pale imitation of one which gravity and the tilt of the deck would produce. Honeyburn wished he could make it a full-scale exercise, firing at a target, but since he was required to account precisely for every shot fired he would have to pay the costs of this indulgence himself and he could not afford it. However, three shots from a newly-mounted stern-chaser could certainly be justified, he told himself; the long six should have its test-firing presently.

'Gun-captains take your orders from me.' He took his watch from his pocket. 'Level your gun. Out tompion. Run out. Prime. Point your gun. Fire!'

The gun-captains went through the motions of applying slow-match to touch-hole, the hands at the side-tackles released them, the guns ran in until they were checked by the breechings.

'Stop vents. Sponge your gun. Load cartridge. Shot your gun –'

And so to the second command to fire. Three-and-a-half minutes between shots; not nearly good enough.

'Secure tackles. Mr Trapp, please to draw three six-pounder cartridges from the magazine and bring them aft – slow-match and tub, too. Mr Sholto, rouse out an empty cask for a target, if you please. Garroway, Peters, Timmis, Johns – aft here and man the six-pounder.'

The four seamen who came running along the deck had manned one of *Cracker*'s bow-chasers in her fight with *Lexington*.

'Off spray-cover and stand to your gun,' said Honeyburn. 'Mr Fitzjames! Muster the hands aft, if you please.'

He took a 6-pounder ball from the ready-use netting and was rejecting it for a more perfect sphere when Mr Trapp and Parkin arrived, the carpenter carrying the canvas-bagged charges and the boy the wooden tub with the smoking slow-match lodged in the niche on its rim. The boatswain brought an empty beef-cask and at Honeyburn's word tossed it over the stern, where it bobbed and receded between the widening white furrows of the wake. The four men of the gun-crew stood waiting; Timmis had taken the sponge-and rammer from its rack.

'Very well,' Honeyburn said. 'Peters, you're gun-captain as before but I'll lay her myself. Stand by to load at my word. Mr Fitzjames, I'll thank you to pay attention,' he added sharply.

The 18-pounder crews had come aft and were crowded abaft the mainmast. Fitzjames was at the lee rail, gazing with studied indifference at the horizon.

'Aye aye, sir,' he growled, turning in leisurely fashion.

'Hear this, now,' said Honeyburn, ignoring him and addressing the men. 'Your carronades can hit hard but only inside a thousand yards range. This fellow –' he slapped the rump of the 6-pounder – 'can hit hard at two thousand yards.' He had his watch in his hand as he spoke. 'We're making ten knots which is a sea-mile in six minutes, and I'm going to fire at one mile range.' He turned away, his eye on the watch. 'Ready – load!'

The swift economical movements of a practised gun-crew were as pleasing to his eye as any *corps de ballet*. When the loaded gun was run out Honeyburn crouched to peer along its barrel, adjusted the quoin a trifle, snapped an order that resulted in the rear wheels of the gun-truck being shifted half-an-inch, and leaped aside with a simultaneous shout.

'Fire!'

Peters's match was at the touch-hole as the word left his lips. The gun flashed and roared and flew back against its restraining ropes, and at once the furious yet controlled movements of sponging and reloading began. The smoke blew to leeward in time for Honeyburn, leaning from the rail, to see the brief white splash – dead in line but some fathoms short of the tiny black speck on the blue astern. Again he crouched to adjust the quoin, trying to allow for the increasing range as well as for those few fathoms; this was Honeyburn's *métier* and at such moments he felt almost inspired. There was no flash to be seen when the smoke of the second discharge drifted aside but he was certain it was over the target. No need for the quoin adjustment – the opening range would do it.

'Fire!' – and after a breathless instant the satisfying sight, far distant but undeniable, of a puff of black fragments.

There was a deal of luck in it as Honeyburn well knew, but he could not admit it even to himself. This was good gunnery. He turned a face red and grinning with triumph on the assembled hands, but the grin vanished as he caught sight of Fitzjames. The lieutenant, hands behind back, was staring idly up at the mainmast crosstrees with his shoulder turned to the activities on the quarterdeck. Honeyburn ground his teeth and choked back the angry reprimand.

'Very well,' he said crisply. 'Carronade crews back to your guns and stand-to. Six-pounder crew secure. Mr Fitzjames, you'll take charge of gun-drill at the eighteen-pounders, if you please. I want twenty rounds fired from each gun and I want it done within forty-five minutes.'

'Aye aye, sir.'

There was a weary resignation in the tone of that response that angered Honeyburn extremely. His patience was almost exhausted; somehow Fitzjames would have to be taught a lesson, and that soon. The crowd of hands trotted for'ard to their guns; the stern-chaser, sponged and secured, disappeared beneath its spray-cover. Sholto, pausing as he left the quarterdeck, spoke diffidently.

'By your leave, sir – I never see better shooting nor that.'

Honeyburn felt cheered. 'The third shot was a lucky one, Mr Sholto,' he said disingenuously. 'Nevertheless, it's that sort of gunnery that will take the place of your ship-to-ship cannonades in the future.'

With the quarterdeck to himself he paced up and down while *Cracker*, her deck vibrating to the incessant rumble of the gun-trucks, sailed steadily onwards under the noonday sun. The need for some form of sight, perhaps a brass point on the muzzle and a ring on the breech; accurate counteraction of the ship's movement, such as a pendulum geared to a delicate elevating mechanism; powder charges exact to a grain and shot moulded to smooth and perfect spheres. In such considerations he had forgotten the problem of Fitzjames when the masthead lookout hailed.

'Deck, there! Sail, stabb'd bow, sir.'

'What do you make of her?' shouted Honeyburn.

'Barca longa, sir, I reckon.' A pause. 'Headin' southerly under low sail, seemin'ly.'

'How far?'

''Bout three mile, sir.'

'Barca longa' was the British seaman's name for any sizeable single-masted fishing vessel in these waters, whether French or Spanish. Commonly they were to be seen by the score a few miles off the coasts, but it was rare to come upon one as far out to sea as this. Fishing-boats of all nations had enjoyed a kind of agreed neutrality throughout the long war with Bonaparte, and though British warships often enough waylaid a French fishing craft it was always for the fresh food she carried and that food was always paid for. Honeyburn had a keen recollection of the fish they had bought from a barca longa off Çorunna on *Cracker*'s second voyage to Spain and his mouth watered at the memory. Pilcardas, they'd been called, little silver fish that were very ambrosia fried and piping hot. It would be worth a golden guinea to provide a treat for himself and his crew.

He went to the starboard rail, hoisted himself onto it by the shrouds, and took out his glass. It was a Dollond bequeathed to him by Michael Fitton, and the round of the lens showed a clear picture of the barca longa in spite of the noonday haze.

'Bear away a point and close the vessel yonder,' he told the man at the wheel.

A longer look through the glass told him why the lookout had thought the fishing-boat to be under low sail. Her big mainsail – she was cutter-rigged – had its peak to the masthead, but from the top of the mast a long spar extended, a spar more than half as long as the mast itself. As he looked, the spar wavered and vanished, lowered to the deck. Some dodge of the offshore fishermen, thought Honeyburn, dismissing it. But what port was she out of? Arcachon was the nearest, and that was fifty or sixty miles away. *Cracker* was steadily overhauling her.

On the gun-brig's deck the rumble of the gun-trucks ceased and Fitzjames's deep voice sounded: 'All guns secure! Jump to it, you lazy sodomites!' Honeyburn could see the man at the massive tiller of the barca longa now, and other men in her stern staring at the approaching warship.

'Mr Sholto! Slacken away sheets!'

Cracker's canvas billowed and flapped as she edged up on the smaller vessel until she was running level, the fishing-boat's stern within easy hail of her quarterdeck. Honeyburn mustered his rusty French.

'*Holà, monsieur le capitaine!*'

One of the brown-faced men at the rail answered. 'I am the captain, monsieur.'

'From what port are you?'

There was a pause before the reply, and in it Honeyburn heard, to his annoyance, Fitzjames exercising his French in conversation with a Frenchman in the barca longa's bows.

'From Arcachon,' shouted the fishing-boat's captain.

'You have a catch? I'll buy pilcardas from you.'

'*Hélas*! We have caught no fish at all, monsieur.' The captain shrugged and spread his hands. 'We sail far out here to look for them because we find no fish closer inshore, *vous comprenez*. But Saint Peter has not been kind.'

The gun-brig was beginning to draw ahead. On an impulse Honeyburn shouted a last question.

'That spar at your masthead, captain – was that to help you search for the shoals?'

Again there was a pause, followed by a curiously indecisive answer. '*Oui, monsieur – mais non, non – c'était un petit expériment, une voile nouvelle –*'

The wind and increasing distance bore the rest away.

'Bear up,' said Honeyburn to the helmsman. 'Sheets, Mr Sholto!'

He waved an arm in parting salute to the receding barca longa and as *Cracker* settled on her old course turned with a frown to face Fitzjames, who had come aft to the quarterdeck.

'Mr Fitzjames,' he said sharply, 'in the future you'll not overstep your duty by conversing with another vessel as you did just now. That is an order.'

'Aye aye, sir,' said Fitzjames, glowering at him. 'But it's my duty to report to you that two French seamen I spoke to declared that their vessel was from a port called, I believe, Cabreton, or something like it. I heard her captain tell you she was from Arcachon.'

The springs of decision are deep below the surface of a man's mind; quite possibly Honeyburn's resolve took shape when he heard these words. At the moment, however, it was indecision that he showed. Beyond the thought that this was the longest utterance he had yet heard from Fitzjames was this mention of Cap Breton, the key name, as it were, of Mad McCormick's theories and his own recurrent speculations upon them.

'Very well, Mr Fitzjames,' he said abruptly, and strode to the after rail to stare at the fishing-boat.

She was already far astern and had altered course eastward across *Cracker*'s wake. Should he put about, make her heave-to and question her captain more searchingly? These seeming oddities, the barca longa being unusually far from land and the matter of the tall spar so hastily lowered from her masthead – they were of little significance after all. And to conclude that her captain had lied about her port of origin was to go too fast; the French seamen Fitzjames had spoken with might have meant simply that they themselves hailed from Cap Breton. He turned away and began to pace the deck, frowning.

Timmis came trotting aft to the wooden belfry on the starboard rail and struck eight bells on the worn brass bell. Noon. Honeyburn, still frowning, went below to his cabin and spread the chart on the table, with pad and pencil to hold it down. There was leeway to be allowed for, the doubtful effect of the current which (according to Mr Trapp) ran northward up this coast; he pencilled figures on the pad, laid his rulers across the chart, fixed his position as precisely as he could. A noon sight, he told himself reprovingly, could have checked his dead-reckoning but he had left it too late. *Cracker*, according to calculation, was 64 sea-miles north-west by north of Cap Breton. The wind holding, she could make 7 knots under easy sail. The moon was in her last quarter. It could not be more convenient.

He swept pad and rulers from the chart and it sprang back into its roll with a snap. His decision was made.

Mr Sholto was a man not easily taken aback, but his broad face displayed astonishment when his captain came on deck and issued his curt orders. Royals to be taken in, sheets hauled, *Cracker* to be laid on a new course south-east by south. He quickly hid his surprise, however, and the watch-on-deck sprang to obey his roar. The gun-brig came round towards the wind, bringing it two point for'ard of the port beam, and began to slant in towards the invisible coast of France.

'Mr Fitzjames!' The lieutenant came aft, looking bored as usual. 'We'll walk, if you please.'

They paced up and down twice in silence. At the after rail, out of earshot of the helmsman, Honeyburn halted and faced his junior. It was satisfactory to watch Fitzjames's stubborn moroseness broken at last, to see his jaw drop and his eyes widen, as he heard his senior's terse announcement.

'Mr Fitzjames. I propose to land on the French coast for an hour or two tonight. You will accompany me.'

III

The Hostile Shore

1

Shortly before midnight *Cracker* was standing-in towards the French coast, a black shape riding smoothly on the slight swell of the waves. The night around her was faintly luminous, a radiance from the dimly-seen sliver of moon lightening the dark haze that prevented any possible view of the land ahead. She was close-hauled under topsails and jib only, and there was no sound on board except the low monotonous cry of the leadsman in the bows.

'No bottom with this line ... no bottom with this line.'

Honeyburn was standing motionless, hands behind back, a little abaft the wheel. A few paces from him at the port rail was the dark figure of Lieutenant Fitzjames, equally motionless. For'ard were the little groups of waiting men: Sholto with the anchor party, Gomez and Peters with the cock-boat ready for launching, Mr Trapp (his volubility curbed by the general orders for silence) with the hands ready at the sheets. This caution and preparation might have seemed premature, the gun-brig being not yet in soundings; but Honeyburn had taken into consideration the deep shown on the chart, the underwater trench, once the estuary of the Adour, that ran right inshore to the ancient harbour of Cap Breton. On the French chart 124 metres was marked only two miles from the harbour – a depth, roughly, of 60 fathoms. He hoped the leadsman's call meant that they were in this deep-water channel now.

Hoped, because their position was in reality quite uncertain. As he stood silent and unmoving in the darkness his mind was in a turmoil of doubt and unease.

Henry Honeyburn was by nature a cautious man; his ten years with the Royal Navy had made him a dutiful if not very efficient naval officer. His decision taken earlier that day, in opposition to both these characteristics, had been prompted by a conjunction of circumstances none of which would singly have led to such an action. There was McCormick's theory, not quite baseless, that some kind of enemy action was in preparation at or near Cap Breton; it had been lurking and nagging at the back of his mind for three days. Then the encounter with the barca longa and her small oddities. These would not have changed his course but for the fact of *Cracker*'s remarkably fast passage from Portsmouth. Here he was within half-a-day's sail of his destination on the night of the 18th, and Captain Page had expected him to arrive 'by the twenty-first' – he could afford a slight divergence from his course, a few hours spent in what might conceivably be a useful reconnaissance, and still reach Orio a day before Page's date.

There was another factor which was perhaps more powerful than Honeyburn would have cared to admit. A night landing on the enemy's coast would show young Fitzjames that his commanding officer was not the over-cautious dotard he seemed to think him.

The plan of action was simple enough and involved no great hazard. He would land at midnight or thereabouts on the beach north or south of Cap Breton, gain the rank of tall dunes he knew to rise beyond high-water mark, find a crest whence he could spy out the land behind them and the neighbourhood of the little port. Sunrise was five hours after midnight but long before that there would be enough light for his survey and he would have retreated to the waiting boat and regained *Cracker* before the sun was up. Conditions were ideal for such a foray. The easterly wind had moderated a trifle, the sea was so slight that the cockboat would have no trouble in landing, there was just enough light for finding a way up the dunes and not enough to make the gun-brig conspicuous if, improbably, there was anyone on the lookout ashore. The low-lying haze, indeed, made *Cracker* quite invisible from the shore. And Honeyburn hadn't allowed for the haze. He had counted on being able to see the line of dunes against the sky as he came in, in all likelihood detecting the break in them denoting the Cap Breton inlet, and selecting his landing-place accordingly. Instead he was approaching blindly from a doubtfully-established position, uncertain whether he was north or south of Cap Breton and entirely dependent on soundings which had not yet come to his aid. With every minute of *Cracker*'s progress towards a hostile shore he was increasingly conscious of his rashness. Had it not been for Fitzjames (though he would not have admitted this) he would have yielded to prudence and turned back.

'Bottom,' called the leadsman, and then, at the next swing, 'by the mark twenty.'

A steep-to shallowing, then; probably they were crossing the rim of the deep-water channel.

'And a half seventeen ... deep sixteen ... by the mark fifteen.'

The wind was a mere breeze now. They were getting the lee of the land. Honeyburn's ear detected the deep murmur in the darkness ahead – breakers on a beach, but of no great size, he thought. His doubts had fled. He was going through with it.

'Deep fourteen ... deep twelve ...'

The French chart marked seventeen metres – say nine fathoms – less than a mile out. The tide was nearing the top of the flood.

'Quarter less ten,' called the leadsman.

'Stand by to let go, Mr Sholto.'

'Aye aye, sir.'

'Deep eight,' the leadsman intoned.

'Bring her to the wind,' Honeyburn told the helmsman.

'Mr Sholto! Let go! Tops'ls in, Mr Trapp.'

The anchor splashed from the bows, *Cracker*'s topsails flapped as she began to gather sternway. Then the fluke bit into good holding-ground and she brought up with a gentle jerk, to ride comfortably to her cable. The cock-boat slapped down onto the slow heave of the waves and Gomez and Peters climbed down into her.

'Come along then, Mr Fitzjames,' said Honeyburn; a boyish excitement was rising in him but he managed to keep his tone even and businesslike.

Fitzjames bestrode the rail and swung himself down to the boat.

'Expect us on board about sunrise, Mr Sholto,' Honeyburn said as he prepared to follow.

'Aye aye, sir. And – good luck, sir.' Sholto's voice in the darkness sounded doubtful.

Honeyburn joined Fitzjames on the stern thwart, Gomez shoved off, and the cock-boat pulled away, rising and falling on the low smooth hills of water. In half-a-dozen strokes the gun-brig was a shadow on the luminescent grey of the night-haze; in another half-dozen she had vanished. Honeyburn had to fight down a return of his qualms. With Sholto in charge, he told himself, *Cracker* was in safe hands, far safer than if he had left Fitzjames in command. And he was resolved not to venture into any situation that could possibly result in their being captured; the coast between Bayonne and Cap Breton, he believed, was virtually an uninhabited desert of sand and marsh, and so was the coast north of Cap Breton – he had yet to learn which part of it he had reached – so they were very unlikely to encounter any human being at this hour of the night.

Unlikely or not, however, he had taken precautions. Both he and Fitzjames were in naval uniform so as to avoid the possibility of being shot as spies. They carried no weapons, and the only thing in Honeyburn's pockets was his Dollond glass. Fitzjames demurred at their landing weaponless – his only comment on his senior's brief explanation of his purpose.

'There is a rumour that the French are building vessels somewhere on this part of the coast, Mr Fitzjames. We may be able to confirm it, or we may see nothing. In any case we shall incur no risk except the very small one of taking a look from the top of the tallest sand-dune we can find.'

'Sword and pistols, sir?' Fitzjames had asked, his grey eyes gleaming.

'No. They would be both useless and a nuisance. If by some unlucky chance we are seen we run like hares for the boat. You understand?'

'Yes, sir.'

And Fitzjames had reverted to his usual sulky silence. He was silent now, sitting close against Honeyburn in the cock-boat's sternsheets since the narrow thwart forced him to do so. Honeyburn could feel the slight tremor of his arm, the tension of excitement; and some of the half-forgotten excitement of his own youthful adventures awoke in him. The rhythmic snoring of the waves breaking on the beach was close ahead now, and there was a dark silhouette, as of much greater waves, rising on the pale blur of the sky – the dunes. The silhouette hardened as the boat swooped over the shoreward waves and he could see no break in its long peaked line. Flecks of white rose and fell on the black of the waves.The surge and retreat of the surf was in his ears.

'Pull starboard!' he said sharply. 'Steady – now, together and roundly.'

The oarsmen sent their craft surging forward on a wavecrest, boated oars as she plunged on in the shallow cataract of surf, and leaped overside to haul her bows onto firm sand. Honeyburn stepped over the gunwale, ankle-deep in retreating foam, and Fitzjames followed. As far as the uncertain light allowed them to see, a wide empty beach stretched away into obscurity on either hand between the line of breaking waves and the dark rank of dunes that rose above; the beach sloped gently up to the dunes, and though it was not far short of high water there was a big stretch of sand to cross to gain their base. Down here by the water's edge there was no wind at all, so complete was the lee given by the miniature mountain-range of sand.

'Shift her with the tide,' Honeyburn said to Gomez. 'No one will come along before we return, but if our luck's out and you're questioned you know what to say.'

'Yes, sir. I answers in Spanish. We're off a *guarda costa* as is anchored out yonder. Brought the captain ashore to stretch 'is legs.'

Honeyburn had been unable to think of a better story, but he thought it highly improbable that it would be needed.

'Very well,' he said. 'Look to see us half-an-hour before sunrise. Mr Fitzjames, follow me.'

'Wait, sir – if you please.'

Fitzjames added the three words as an afterthought. He was gazing along the beach to southward, funnelling his eyes with his hands to increase their vision. Honeyburn could see nothing but the faint outlines lost in night and haze at three hundred paces distance.

'What is it?' he demanded impatiently.

'Three shapes – they could be huts – in a row. Close to the dunes.'

Honeyburn dragged his glass from his pocket. All he could make out was a shifting blur; but if there were huts there, so close to the boat –

'We had better investigate,' he said, and set off along the beach with Fitzjames a pace behind.

His course took them slanting up the sand and in fifty paces they were treading fine shingle. He led the way rightward, to bring sand underfoot again; if these were huts, fishermen's dwellings perhaps, their owners might be asleep in them. The last thing he wanted to do was to alert inquisitive natives. Already his thoughts were running on what he must do if these huts were inhabited. They would have to move the boat farther northward –

'I believe they have wheels,' said Fitzjames behind him.

The three dark blotches, close to each other in a neat rank, were perfectly visible to Honeyburn now but he could discern no wheels. He went on without stopping, his gaze fixed on the objects ahead, wishing his eyes were as good as his young companion's. Fifty yards farther on he stopped dead.

'You're right!' he exclaimed, his voice betraying excitement. 'They *have* wheels. These are gun-carriages, Mr Fitzjames – field-pieces – and where there are guns there are artillerymen. We must –'

'They're bathing-machines, sir.' Fitzjames sounded mildly apologetic.

'Bathing –' Honeyburn focussed his glass. 'Good gracious! So they are!'

He had seen bathing-machines at Weymouth, where King George had made them fashionable before his wits left him altogether. Horses pulled them into waist-deep seawater so that the occupant could step down modestly and directly for his or her dip. There were hundreds in busy use along the south coast of England on an August day, and there was no reason why the French shouldn't indulge in sea-bathing on this unthreatened coast of the Landes. But bathing-machines, even only three of them, implied the neighbourhood of a resort, a town or village. And something else.

'They were brought here by horses,' he said, 'and that means a road for vehicles, or a track at the least, coming through the dunes. I fancy I can see its point of emergence, a little beyond those machines. We give that track a wide berth. Come along.'

He turned and led the way up the beach, bearing left to increase their distance from the bathing-machines. A belt of shingle underfoot, a trudge through soft loose sand, and the bulky mass of the dunes towered above their heads. He paused a moment, tilting his head back to squint up at the half-seen facets and clefts, all smoothly rounded, and then started to climb a steeply-angled trough that wound upward toward the paler sky.

Sand filled his shoes and slid under his tread. At every laborious step half his effort was lost in the backward slide. In thirty seconds his breath was coming in gasps and he had to slow his first enthusiastic efforts. It was some comfort to hear a grunt or two behind him, indicating that Fitzjames wasn't finding it easy. The trough bent leftward and rose steeply to a crescent ridge of sand tufted with marram-grass; on the other side of the ridge was an equally steep drop into a cup-shaped hollow beyond which another trough climbed to vanish round a corner of the mountain of sand rising high on his left. He trod gingerly along the ridge, the marram-grass pricking his legs, and launched himself at the flank of the sand-mountain.

There was no wind here among the dunes and the sand gave out the warmth it had absorbed from the long day's sun. He sweated as he struggled; and the struggle was vain. The angle was too high, and though he burrowed with his hands for hold, filling his coat-sleeves to the elbows with sand, he merely slid down again in the furrows he had dug. He let himself slip back to the ridge-crest.

'Better try across the slope, sir,' suggested Fitzjames, who had wisely made no attempt to follow his captain.

'I was – about – to do so,' Honeyburn panted.

Traversing the slope of the dune was easier. They slid down a foot or so at every step but they made progress, and beyond the steep corner was an easier slope leading round to the left. They entered a narrow valley with shadowy peaks on either hand. Honeyburn, who had recovered his breath, resisted the temptation to go as fast as he could; it would be an hour and more before there was any sign of dawn. The valley bent to the right and ended in a rising bank joining two loftier mounds, a bank so high that its dark barrier obscured most of the feeble light of the sky overhead. It was steep, but not too steep to climb, though the toil was more than doubled by the continual and exasperating slither and recovery. At its top, on the rounded crest spanning the gap between two ascending slopes on either hand, Honeyburn paused to take breath and reflect.

They had already climbed well over a hundred feet above sea-level, and they had penetrated a considerable way inland from the shore. The height he had expected; the French chart had marked the height of one sand-dune as 100 metres, more than 300 feet, and named it as 'Mont Pilat'. But that was the chart's only indication of the dunes, and – lacking a map – he had unthinkingly assumed that there was a single ridge of sand-formed crests between the foreshore and the flat marshes inland. It was, he now realised, a quite unwarrantable assumption. There was evidently a broad belt of dunes that might take them a long time to cross. They could hardly lose themselves, for even in the valleys of the dunes they could hear the murmur of the surf; all they had to do when the time came to retreat was to head towards the sound of the sea. And there was no need to return by the way they had come, which in any case would be difficult to find. There would be no hazards in the shape of cliffs or chasms among these mountains of sand, and if it was advisable to dodge round a very steep slope rather than try to climb it, the descent of one involved only a safe and rapid slide. Their retreat was assured. It was the advance that was doubtful.

'May I ask, sir, where we are heading for?' said Fitzjames beside him.

His voice was respectful enough, but Honeyburn darted a suspicious glance at him. Fitzjames, however, was no more than a faceless silhouette against the paler sandhills.

'For a high dune,' he said shortly; and then, realising that he owed his companion more explanation than that, added 'a dune that will afford a view over the countryside beyond as soon as there's light enough.'

'Perhaps, sir, the dune yonder would serve,' Fitzjames said.

It was not too dark to see his outstretched arm. Above and to their left a shadowy dome appeared above the intervening dips and curves of sand. It was plainly a good deal higher than their present position.

'If we climbed the slope east of us,' said Fitzjames, 'we might find a way –'

'Yes,' Honeyburn said, and started to climb the slope.

It was a long climb, and before he reached its stop he could hear the night wind hissing in the marram-grass that fledged the crest. That steady east wind, blowing in his face as he topped the rise, was welcome not only for its cooling effect but also for its assurance that they had reached the summit-ridges of this strange upland. There were more humps and hollows on its farther side and he could make out that they decreased in height but not what lay beyond them. The higher dome showed itself to northward, apparently quite close. The ridge they had gained seemed to lead to it, and Honeyburn began to walk along the ridge, with the wind cool on his right cheek.

It was farther than he had thought and involved a good deal of ploughing uphill and slithering down, but the route was never in doubt. He was able to give some thought to the question of where they were. The bathing-machines and their corollary a road through the dunes suggested the neighbourhood of Bayonne, the only place other than Cap Breton that was named on the French chart. But Bayonne was a good twelve miles south of Cap Breton, and four miles from the coast; he was certain his dead-reckoning hadn't taken him so far south. A mental check of his calculations inclined him to feel fairly sure that they had not landed north of Cape Breton but some little way south of it, perhaps a mile or more. With luck, the tall dune might command a northward prospect of the Cap Breton inlet and its surroundings.

When they arrived at the base of the final uprising of

sand it was evident that the steep-sided dome had been the end-on view of a hog's-back ridge. Up this they toiled, the wind increasing in strength as they climbed, and reached the arching crest of its summit. As far as could be seen in the obscurity of the hazy night it was indeed the highest point in this part of the dunes; but to northward, whither Honeyburn's eager gaze went at once, the jumble of summits and ridges seemed to continue at only a slightly lesser height until the darkness hid them, with no sign of the gap that must occur where Cap Breton lay. He sighed and turned to look eastward.

Here the view (if such it could be called when it consisted of planes of black and grey) was at least a wide one. From their feet the sand-slope fell steeply away, humped into dunes and furrowed by gullies but descending to a vast dark floor that appeared to stretch unbroken into the night, a plain that for all they could see of its details might have been the sea two hundred feet below them. Straining his sight to the uttermost, Honeyburn thought he could make out a glimmer here and there that suggested water, and patches of lighter darkness that could be areas of sand. Fitzjames, who had been silent since their last halt, spoke.

'With your leave, sir – if we're to stay up here till dawn it would be as well to get out of the wind. I could kick out a scoop a fathom below the crest on the lee side.'

'Yes,' Honeyburn said; it was a sensible suggestion and impelled him to take his lieutenant further into his confidence. 'But to stay here won't fulfil my purpose, Mr Fitzjames. I believe Cap Breton to lie north of us, a mile perhaps. I must overlook it, or at least the countryside immediately behind it. We must go on.'

'A mile, through these bloody – I beg your pardon, sir,' Fitzjames interrupted himself solemnly. 'Allow me to suggest an alternative. If you got on top of the dune down yonder – the fellow sticking up from a sort of headland – you might see round the corner, so to speak.'

He was pointing down the slope below them as he spoke. Strenuous exercise or the novelty of their situation had broken down his artificial barrier of reserve and he continued with mounting enthusiasm.

'These dunes don't make a regular row on this side like they do on the seaward side. You can make out how they stand forward in a big promontory – it might be the bows of a ship and this dune we're on the foremast. See the hump I mean, sir? The line of the sandhills falls sharp back on the port hand and we'd likely see past them to this Cap Breton place.'

Honeyburn could see the ghostly pallor of the dunes descending to encroach on the blackness of the plain. On the right of this steep promontory, as well as on its left, their line fell back seaward, and it occurred to him that the narrowing of the dune-belt that this implied could indicate the Cap Breton gap to northward and the road penetrating to the beach to southward. The hump Fitzjames was pointing out was the last eminence of any height on the promontory and must be little more than fifty feet above the level of the plain. It was an even chance, he thought, whether or not he would be able to see anything of Cap Breton from it; and it had been no part of his plan to descend so near the marshes of the Landes. On the other hand, he was no more anxious than Fitzjames to struggle through another mile or more of steep-angled sand – and their time was limited. The dawn must be close at hand by now.

'Very well,' he said. 'Down we go.'

With Fitzjames following, he plunged down the yielding slope, digging in his heels and balancing with difficulty on the sliding surface. A saddle, a falling ridge, a traverse across a face of sand and another long slide, brought them to a neck where the marram-grass grew thick. A short steep scramble and they were on top of the dune they had aimed for. Here was no peak of sand but a lumpy little tableland of deep hollows. Fitzjames's analogy, Honeyburn thought as he peered round him, was apt enough; it was like being in the bows of a ship putting out from land, for on either hand the dark sea of the plain – marsh or grass, he couldn't see which – rolled back to lap against the feet of the dunes. Northward in the direction of Cap Breton there was as yet nothing to be seen but darkness and the pallid barrier of sand. But now that he was lower down he could plainly see the gleam of a pool some way out below him, and a shape that must be a stunted tree even farther away. And – surely the eastern sky was lightening through the haze, and a pale streak growing low above the plain.

'Dawn, Mr Fitzjames,' he said with satisfaction. 'In a few minutes we shall be able –'

He stopped abruptly. Startling in its clarity, there came from no great distance to southward the note of a bugle.

2

The immediate reaction of both officers was to crouch below the fringe of wind-blown marram-grass that rimmed the hollow where they were standing, though there was no possibility of their being seen. The bugle had sounded very like the huntsman's blast signalling a 'view'.

'Can't be for us,' Fitzjames said; he lay on his chest to peer above the rim. 'Look, sir – a light. And another.'

The lights were like tiny lanterns strung across the darkness; a third and a fourth winked into sight. They could be anything from a mile to half-a-mile away and they were close together in a horizontal line.

'Tents!' exclaimed Fitzjames. 'The lights are in a row of tents, sir.'

Honeyburn had just come to the same conclusion. 'Precisely,' he said, 'a detachment of the military. The bugle was sounding their revally.'

McCormick's description of this countryside as 'naught but marshes and lagoons' was something wide of the mark, he thought resentfully. Here were not only roads leading to bathing-machines but also army encampments. An idea struck him. If the French were indeed preparing some attack to seaward and constructing vessels hereabouts, they might well have soldiers guarding their operations. Could it be that he was much nearer to Cap Breton than he had thought?

'Those Frogs are eating their breakfast, likely enough,' said Fitzjames; he sounded a trifle envious.

'We'll get ours when we've seen what they're about.' Honeyburn settled himself more comfortably, with his chin on the sandy rim. 'We wait, Mr Fitzjames, and we watch carefully.'

The fast-growing light was beginning to reveal more of their surroundings. With every passing minute fresh details of the landscape emerged from the paling greyness of early morning, and against the widening bar of dawn sky the vast plain of the Landes showed a long black horizon as straight as a ruled line. Spreading eastward from the promontory of sand where they lay was the kind of desolate country Honeyburn had mentally pictured: patches of reedy marshes where wisps of mist lay above glimmering waters, sandy stretches, areas of what appeared to be dry turf where a few bushes and low trees grew. Away on his left where this wilderness was bordered by the perspective of the dunes he could see nothing to suggest the proximity of Cap Breton – if indeed the place lay in that direction.

But it was in the opposite direction, southward, that the gaze of the watchers was chiefly fixed, for here, now, the encampment and the stir of movement there could be seen. A score of small tents were ranged on a slight rise a mile away and Honeyburn could see the ant-like figures of men passing to and fro. A further mile away, beyond the encampment and appearing to its left, a church steeple thrust up its thin black wedge against the lightening sky – a village, then, standing a mile or two inland from the bastions of the dunes. He could make out the cluster of houses and what seemed to be a larger building, a château perhaps, a short distance apart from them. He saw, too, that the whitish streaks he had taken for water were in fact a road. It was no more than a narrow unfenced lane appearing and vanishing as it twisted between the marshy patches, but now he knew what it was he could trace its course from the distant village to pass not far from the row of tents and run northward parallel to the line of dunes, crossing a bare half-mile from their lookout-post on the promontory dune. There was light enough now to mark its thin white line winding away to the left towards the invisible – and still hypothetical – Cap Breton.

Again the bugle sang shrilly from the camp but Honeyburn heard it with half an ear. He was at last able to form in his mind a sketch-map of his probable position. *There's bound to be a track of sorts connecting Cap Breton with Bayonne*, McCormick had said. This road must run from Bayonne northward along the inland side of the dunes, through the village yonder, and on to Cap Breton with its little harbour in the gap of the dunes. A lane branching westward from it – probably from the village with the church spire – crossed the dunes to the seashore where they had seen the bathing-machines. In all this there was no definite evidence to support McCormick's theory; but if the soldiers from the camp were to march down the road towards Cap Breton it would at least suggest that they were going to relieve a military guard watching over some naval construction there.

The eastern sky was aglow with light now, and the light was taking on the pale golden tint that presaged sunrise. Fitzjames had not spoken for a long time; possibly he had resolved to reassume the incommunicative attitude which the manoeuvres of the past few hours had made him drop. He didn't speak now, but his uneasy movement and glance at his senior showed that he was aware (as indeed was Honeyburn) that if they were to be back at the boat by sunrise they should have begun the return journey before now. But Honeyburn's gaze was intent on the distant soldiery, for they were moving.

The bugle-call had initiated a bustle of movement by the tents, the ant-like figures resolving themselves into two companies which appeared as two short ribbons of green and white. The ribbons moved rightward, towards the road. Honeyburn, watching through his glass, felt a twinge of disappointment when the leaders of the first column marched straight across the road and headed over the broken ground towards the dunes. Then he was shaken by the sudden realisation that if they were making for the shore they must see the boat. But if that was where they were going they would surely have marched by the track from the village – and the second column, at least, had wheeled onto the road and was marching along it towards him, led by an officer on horseback. It was time, and more than time, to go.

'Come along then, Mr Fitzjames,' he said briskly, cramming the glass into his pocket. 'We'll make sail while we may.' He had started to scramble to his feet when he realised that the crest of the dune and its southern flank were in full view of the approaching soldiers. 'If we crawl to the edge and get onto the north side,' he said, crouching again, 'we can do it.'

The sound of a horse's hooves came to his ears as he spoke and he turned to look cautiously at the road. The officer had urged his mount to a canter and was coming on ahead of the troop. He was already less than half-a-mile away; in a few minutes he would be past the promontory of sand, with its north flank open to his view.

'H'm,' said Honeyburn, frowning and rubbing his chin. 'We'd better wait until they're past and then get up by way of the south flank, after all.'

It was full daylight now and he observed with some annoyance a faint grin, quickly vanishing, on his companion's face.

'Aye aye, sir,' said Fitzjames gravely.

They resumed their watch. It was safe enough, with the fringing marram-grass to conceal their heads. The officer came cantering on; a grey-whiskered man in a uniform of light blue with silver facings, as Honeyburn's glass showed him. He reined in opposite the projecting dune, whose frontal slope ran out in a bank sparsely overgrown with prickly shrubs which merged into the five or six hundred yards of rough ground that lay between it and the road. For a moment Honeyburn fancied that they had been seen, for the officer seemed to be staring straight at him; but the man's gaze passed on as he scanned the rising gullies and mounds of the wall of sand above them. Then he wheeled his horse and raised an arm apparently in signal to the marching troop, after which he remained where he was. Behind and beyond him rays of bright gold reached up from the horizon.

Honeyburn, chafing at this delay, anxiously weighed the chances of making a dash for it. They could get unseen down to the saddle behind their dune, between it and the next and higher mound, but for the further ascent of a hundred feet or so they would be in sight of the road. A man on horseback couldn't follow them; but the officer over there had fifty men in his command and they carried muskets. To wait until the troop had gone on at least a quarter of a mile along the road was the merest prudence, though it meant regaining the waiting boat long after the time he had told Gomez to expect them.

It seemed an unconscionable time before the marching men came round the curve of the narrow road – to halt untidy, at a yell from a sergeant, a few yards short of the horseman. The sergeant came forward and conferred with the officer, both glancing up at the dunes; the officer consulted a watch which he produced from the breast of his tunic and nodded at the sergeant, who turned and shouted at the men; the men broke ranks and made themselves comfortable at the roadside, some standing talking in groups and others sitting down. It looked as if they proposed to stay there for some time. And the rim of the sun rose blinding bright above the horizon-line.

'Sir,' Fitzjames said in a low voice. 'The glass – the sun reflected from it could give us away.'

Honeyburn nodded and put the glass in his pocket. Fitzjames was perfectly right, of course, and it was unreasonable to feel annoyed. He had noted that the French soldiers were an oddly-dressed lot, half of them in green jackets and white breeches which in many cases were a very bad fit and the other half in countrified civilian clothing. Some had muskets and the rest had sticks or short poles as substitutes. All of them, he thought, looked very young. They were cheerful enough, and the sergeant's bark was heard at intervals when the talk and laughter rose too loud. The sun climbed clear of the horizon and its heat began to make itself felt.

For the two on the dune-top there was nothing to be done but wait until the soldiery moved on. And the soldiery seemed in no hurry to move. Had it not been for the party's somewhat casual air Honeyburn would have begun to wonder whether this was the start of a search for himself and Fitzjames; his mind did, in fact, toy with the unpleasant possibility that Gomez and Peters had been taken and put to the question, a message sent to the encampment, and a systematic combing of the dunes initiated. It was too unlikely to be considered for long. It could only be by chance that the troop had halted right opposite their hiding-place. In their own good time they would resume their march along the road – though if they were going to halt after every mile of marching it would take them some time to reach Cap Breton.

The sun climbed higher, the men in hiding began to sweat in its heat, and still there was no sign of movement on the road. Away to the right across the pale shimmer of the plain the tiled roofs of the village glowed pink. A sudden screeched order brought Honeyburn's attention back to the road, and he let out a grunt of relief; at last they were going to resume their march. The men were back in their ranks and slinging muskets. He saw the officer put a hand to his mouth and a whistle sounded piercingly. Like an echo came the note of a second whistle – and it came from high on the dunes above. The sergeant gave another yell and the whole troop left the road and came plunging across the rough ground, straight for the promontory dune.

In the second of time before the need for action asserted itself Honeyburn realised what was happening. This had nothing to do with Cap Breton and its dubious secret. These were army recruits in training and they were engaging in a mock battle. The first troop had moved north through the dunes to take up position on the miniature heights behind them and they were about to be attacked by the second troop.

He threw a swift glance round him. They were lost if anyone came to the top of this dune; and when the men climbed above it a downward glance would reveal them. Of the several sandy hollows that pitted the little plateau of the dune's summit one was steep-sided and its western rim was overhung by thick marram-grass.

'Follow!' he rapped at Fitzjames, and writhed across to it on his belly.

Below them on either hand as they tumbled into the shallow depression there sounded the grunts and oaths of the French attacking force struggling up the sand, and the sergeant's gasping shout: '*Montez – montez! À gauche, là*!' They plastered themselves against the side of the hollow, getting what cover they could from the marram-grass on its rim. Honeyburn caught a fleeting glimpse of one uniformed man who had come rather higher up the flank than the rest, his slung musket jolting on his shoulders and the long sword-bayonet slapping against his white-breeched thigh as he toiled upwards. Then he was out of sight. The panting breaths and metallic clanking receded, the sergeant's breathless yells sounded more faintly overhead. Honeyburn released pent breath and rose cautiously to his feet.

'The officer,' muttered Fitzjames warningly.

The officer was still sitting his mount on the road, one leg cocked negligently across his saddle-bow. Distant though he was, the brilliant sunlight showed his every movement as he took flint and steel from his sabretache and lit a long black cigar. From beyond the dune-crests above came the crackle of musketry, a ragged volley followed by thin cheering; evidently blank cartridge had been issued to lend verisimilitude to the 'battle'.

Fitzjames had wriggled to the eastward rim and was watching the officer. Honeyburn sat with his back against the warm sand of the hollow and reflected gloomily that they were no more free to move from their position than they had been an hour ago. If they made a dash for it, certain to be seen by the officer and also by the men deployed among the dunes, they were bound to lead the pursuit within sight of the gun-brig and the boat on the shore. Remembering the width of the dune-lands they had crossed, he thought it unlikely that the mock battle would extend itself to the heights fronting the sea whence boat and vessel could be seen; and a second rattle of musketry, sounding no farther away than the first, comfortingly supported this hopeful conclusion. But there was no comfort in the reflection that if Fitzjames and he got clear away (and that still hung in the balance) he would have gained nothing at all by this expedition.

The sun poured into the hollow and he sweated profusely. He had left his watch on board *Cracker* but by the sun's height it must be well into the forenoon watch – mid-morning. Incongruously, considering their situation, he fell into a doze, and came out of it with a start at the sound of Fitzjames's voice.

'The officer's moving off, sir.'

The officer was walking his horse along the road in the direction of the village, to rein-in when he had gone two hundred yards or so and stare up at the dunes. Within a few minutes the watchers saw the forerunners of the returning skirmishers emerging from the sandy recesses to stumble across to the road and form ranks there. It was a relief to see that they had chosen to come down farther along instead of by their way of ascent.

'We could move now, sir,' Fitzjames suggested.

Against the odds, the chance of getting back to the boat unseen had been given them, and Honeyburn, anxious though he was to regain his ship, was not going to jeopardize that chance by premature action.

'No,' he said. 'We wait until they're all down and marching away along that road.'

The wait was longer than he had expected. The sergeants had worried the mob of men into their two troops and they were formed ready for marching, but evidently there was a hitch of some sort. A whistle blew, a long shrill blast, and after a pause another. Then, after a further pause of several minutes, the officer rode to the head of the column and it began to move off, along the road towards the encampment. But two green-uniformed men had been left behind, and these two started to walk back along the road, stopping every few paces to gaze up at the dunes.

Honeyburn could wait no longer. The muskets the two carried were unlikely to fire ball and if they were seen there was no danger; but he was particularly anxious that there should be no chase across the dunes to reveal, as it must do, the presence of boat and ship. If the soldiers on the road didn't advance so far that they could see round the corner of the promontory it would be safe to climb up along its north flank.

'We'll move, Mr Fitzjames,' he said. 'But first I'll reconnoitre the route to make sure we can climb it quickly. Stay here until I hail you, and watch the two down yonder.

Inform me if they move so that they have a view of the gully on the north.'

'Aye aye, sir.'

It was only a drop of a few feet to the short and narrow saddle connecting their dune to the higher bastion of sand that rose behind it, and on the saddle Honeyburn was screened from the road by a projecting shoulder. In front of him now a broad nose mounted steeply and down on his right was the deep trough by which the attacking party had climbed. Round on the sandy slope above the gully was a grass-tufted ledge, seven or eight feet up from where he stood on the saddle. The soldier he had glimpsed from his hiding-place had been climbing up by this ledge, he remembered, and it looked a rather easier way than descending into the trough, which was pitched at a high angle and ploughed up by the passage of fifty pairs of slithering boots.

He scrambled up to the grassy stance with little difficulty and found that he was still hidden from the road by the dune-top below him where Fitzjames lay sprawled peering over the outer rim. And from the ledge a wave or fold of the sand formed a ramp that slanted diagonally up the smooth flank to end just below a scallop of crest that shone pale gold against the blue sky overhead. It shouldn't take them more than five minutes to tread this handy gangway and get safely out of sight beyond the skyline.

Honeyburn turned to call Fitzjames to come on. The grass ledge was not large and slanted slightly outward, so he turned with caution, looking down to ensure the placing of his feet. And he saw the green-uniformed man below him.

The man must have come down the gully, hidden by the bulge of its lower flank. He had no musket and had lost his *képi*, though the sword-bayonet hung in its scabbard from his belt. This – it flashed upon Honeyburn at once – was the laggard for whom the troops had waited, the missing man for whose benefit the whistle had been blown. He was plodding very slowly down the loose sand. If he went on plodding and didn't stop to look up all would be well. Honeyburn stood rigid and motionless on his ledge, holding his breath. Fitzjames's call, low-pitched though it was, sounded shockingly loud to his ears.

'They've halted, sir. One's lit a pipe.'

The soldier in the gully had heard and stopped. If the quick motion of his hand to the hilt of his bayonet was any indication, he had recognised the words as English. Honeyburn, perched like a carved saint in a cathedral niche thirty feet above, saw his instant upward glance and was convinced that he must be seen. But the glance was directed below him and to one side, to the dune-top whence the voice had come. With only the briefest hesitation the soldier began to climb across the sand-slope towards the saddle, quite unaware of the man poised overhead.

Honeyburn's mind worked hard and fast. Clearly the man below had not yet seen his comrades down on the road. At all costs he must not be allowed to give the alarm. To shout a warning to Fitzjames, who had resumed his watch as soon as he had spoken, was equally out of the question. Now the soldier had gained the saddle and was standing, half-crouched, to get his breath. His back was turned on the ledge where Honeyburn stood and he was gazing intently at the short wall of sand that intervened between him and the plateau where Fitzjames lay. He drew the bayonet from its sheath with his left hand, passed it into his right, and took one step forward.

Before he could take another he was flat on his face with Honeyburn's bony knees in his back and Honeyburn's bony fingers round his throat.

3

That flying leap from the ledge had been swiftly gauged and successfully performed. In the exultation of fierce attack Honeyburn hardly noticed the stab of pain in his right knee. The man under him had not been able to utter a sound beyond a choking gurgle but he was writhing furiously and struggling to use the bayonet in his hand. Honeyburn pinned down the hand with his knee and tightened his grip on the man's neck; he was not a muscular man but his long thin fingers were like steel wires and he could lift an 18-pounder ball with finger and thumb. The movement beneath him began to subside.

'What – by God!' Fitzjames's head had appeared over the edge above. 'A Frog! How came he here?'

'Get back to your post,' Honeyburn panted. 'Mark any movement on the road and report to me.'

It was just possible, though unlikely, that the pair waiting below had caught a glimpse of him as he leaped. The body under him went suddenly limp. He got up cautiously and found that he was shaking all over. He had to force himself to stoop and turn the limp head, to assure himself from the ghastly face and protruding tongue that the Frenchman was dead.

Honeyburn had fought his guns in action, had seen men dashed into bloody pulp by enemy shot, but he had never before killed a man in close conflict. Obeying an irresistible impulse, he turned away and was violently sick. While he was thus engaged Fitzjames poked his head over the edge, stared for a moment, and made his report.

'They've not moved, sir – sitting by the wayside. Nothing else on the road.'

Honeyburn turned a wan face. 'Very well, Mr Fitzjames. We'll shape a course for the boat.'

Fitzjames slid down to the saddle and bent to look at the Frenchman. 'Is he dead, sir?'

'Yes.'

'And you're wounded.'

He was pointing to the red stain on his captain's white trousers. Honeyburn pulled up the trouser-leg and revealed an unpleasant-looking gash in the side of the knee; he must have landed with that knee on the bayonet blade.

'I'd better bind it up,' Fitzjames said, pulling a none-too-clean kerchief from his pocket.

'No. Thank you, Mr Fitzjames, but it wouldn't stay in position. It's a flesh-wound and I can manage.'

'He had a bayonet, and you tackled him bare-handed.'

The admiration in the young man's voice irritated Honeyburn.

'He was taken unawares,' he said sharply. 'He came down the gully and never so much as saw me, poor fellow.'

He turned and limped across the sandy neck to begin the climb. Fitzjames, with a puzzled stare and a shake of his head, followed. It was no easy task to gain a footing on the grassy ledge, which had been partly demolished when Honeyburn sprang from it, but once they were over it the slanting ramp on the dune-flank gave faster progress in spite of the invariable downward slide that made double work of every upward step. The pain of Honeyburn's knee was not lessened by this sort of walking and he was glad to rest it for a moment or two when they had reached and crossed the scallop of sand at the head of the gully – glad, too, of the steady breeze that blew up here and cooled his sweat. Still blowing from the east, he was relieved to note; it should fill *Cracker*'s sails as soon as he got on board, and bear him as fast as possible away from the scene of his failed venture.

The humps and dales of the upper dune-lands stretched their weird maze in front and on either hand, but Honeyburn's glance quickly picked out the hog-backed crest from which they had descended, a pale crescent high against the blue and framed between two domes of sand above them. He clenched his teeth against the pain and set a pace that brought much puffing and panting from Fitzjames behind him. It must be approaching noon. Boat and gun-brig would be desperately wondering what action to take.

It was mostly uphill going to reach the neighbourhood of the high dune, winding troughs where the heat was like an oven and ridges where the breeze brought relief, but in bright sunlight there was no difficulty in holding their course. They crossed the nose of sand at the northern foot of the hog's-back and now heard the sound of the sea, though it was still invisible. Honeyburn, limping heavily, held on straight for the sea, threading the sandy maze that had begun to trend downhill, and almost at once the deep-blue bar of the horizon lifted beyond the falling crests. Five minutes more and they were at the top of a wide trough of sand that fell in a hundred-foot slope to run out on the shingle of the beach. There was the gun-brig, at anchor a mile out from the white of the surf; and there was the boat at the edge of the surf, away to the right from the foot of the trough. The shore to southward where they had seen the bathing-machines was not in view, being hidden by the shoulder of the dune that flanked the trough on that side.

Honeyburn's satisfaction at this welcome sight was marred by a horrified perception of his own temerity. He had brought his ship within cannon-shot of an enemy shore (a lee shore, too, in any but these exceptional conditions) and left her anchored there, in broad daylight, for a whole morning; he had gone ashore, taking the only other commissioned officer with him, escaping capture by the narrowest margin and achieving no useful purpose. It was true that the enemy shore was as peaceful a place as any that might be found in Europe, with no forts or batteries to threaten *Cracker*, true also that their encounter with the French soldiers was mere bad luck. But he could imagine how the bald statement of his actions would look in a report, and the incredulous wrath of a senior officer reading it. Failing to make a report would be derogation of duty but it was a risk he resolved there and then to take.

'Wait,' he said to Fitzjames, who was on the point of starting down the slope. 'I'll reconnoitre the beach first.'

He trod round the slope on the left, wincing at each movement of his right leg, until he could see round the shoulder of the dune. The southward stretch of sand was not, as he had hoped, deserted. His glass showed him a bathing-machine axle-deep in the blue water a yard or two beyond the small breaking waves, a short stout woman wearing a broad-brimmed straw hat standing near it above the white line of surf, rather more than a quarter of a mile from the boat. Farther to the left at the base of the sandhills a four-wheeled carriage was standing near the other two bathing-machines with a horse between its shafts, and a second horse was tethered nearby. There were two men sitting on the ground in the patch of shade afforded by the carriage. None of the three persons he could see seemed at all disturbed by the presence of the anchored gun-brig; to a landsman's eye, of course, there was nothing to suggest that she was a British vessel. All he and Fitzjames had to do was to go down to the boat and be taken back on board.

With the certainty of safety there came a sudden collapse of the dogged resolution that had so far upheld him. Edging back round the sandy slope, he felt weak and giddy, and a downward glance at his blood-soaked stocking told him that the wound in his knee was still bleeding fast. Fitzjames was watching him with some concern.

'Down to the boat, Mr Fitzjames,' he said with as much briskness as he could summon. 'Fast as you can go, and have her afloat when I come.'

Following Fitzjames's flying figure down the long trough of sand required a new summoning of determination. Honeyburn told himself glumly that he was getting too old for escapades of this sort; and then remembered that there was reason enough for his faintness in the facts that he had taken no food or drink for fourteen hours, had exerted himself violently under a hot sun, and had lost a considerable amount of blood. When he had staggered nearly to the bottom of the slope he saw Gomez running up the beach towards him. The next thing he was conscious of was being lifted up and set on his feet.

'You're a job for Mr Trapp, sir, seemin'ly,' Gomez was saying; the carpenter was also ship's surgeon. 'Arm across my shoulder, sir. Bear up, now, and we'll get you aboard. – Christ, we was worried, sir,' he went on when they were moving slowly down the beach. ''Eard firin' up where you was. And we was spotted 'ere at the boat, best part of an hour ago. A woman and a young girl comes along the beach from south'ard and asks in French lingo 'oo we was. I answers Spanish like you told me, sir – the girl understood it, I reckon – and after a bit they goes away back again.'

They had reached the water's edge. Fitzjames and Peters had the boat afloat and Gomez heaved his captain bodily into the sternsheets. Fitzjames clambered inboard, the two seamen ran her out through the small breakers and scrambled in over the gunwales, soaked from head to foot, to grasp an oar apiece and pull lustily for the gun-brig. Honeyburn gripped the edge of the thwart beneath him and held himself erect with an effort; he was determined not to disgrace himself by swooning away like a hysterical woman. The sight of the familiar hull and spars growing against the blue sky ahead revived him somewhat and after a moment or two he was able to turn and look at the shore.

They were nearly halfway to the ship now but in the brilliant sunlight he could see every detail. The fat woman on the beach beyond the bathing-machine was waving both arms and appeared to be doing a kind of frenzied dance. She was shouting, too – a thin high wail came to his ears above the sounds of the boat's progress. He had just decided that her performance was no concern of his when another cry, nearer at hand, was heard by all in the boat.

'*À moi*! *À moi*!'

'Someone in the water, port hand,' Fitzjames said, shading his eyes against the glitter of the waves. 'There – right on the beam.'

Honeyburn was in time to see flash of an arm, instantly vanishing, a long stone's throw away. He felt a dull irritation; he needed urgently to get on board *Cracker* and into his cabin where he could collapse privately. But that cry for help couldn't be ignored. He made himself speak sharply.

'Back port, pull starboard. Now – together.'

The boat swung in a ninety-degree arc and surged forward, heading for the spot where they had seen that raised arm. Fitzjames was standing up and gazing ahead.

'There!' he cried again, pointing.

Honeyburn had seen it – the white gleam of something just below the surface a fathom from the bows.

'Hold water!'

The boat wallowed to a stop, rising and falling on the waves. There was no sign of the swimmer. Fitzjames looked at Honeyburn.

'Shall I try if I can get him, sir?'

'Yes, if you can swim.'

A good many naval officers were unable to swim a stroke, but there was no doubting Fitzjames's ability. He tore off his jacket, kicked off his shoes, and dived over the gunwale as smoothly as a seal from a rock. For what seemed a long time, while those in the boat watched the gently-heaving water, there was nothing to be seen. Then, with a gasp and a splutter, his head broke the surface close to the boat's stern, and with it a second head wearing a blue-and-white cap.

Between them they hauled inboard the small limp body, Fitzjames clambering in over the stern after it, and laid it on the floorboards. It was clad in a curious costume of blue striped with white, to match the cap, with frills at neck and knee and elbow. The wet cotton clung closely to a slight but well-formed figure.

'Good gracious!' said Honeyburn. 'It's a girl!'

He had started up from his seat to peer at the rescued swimmer and the movement was his undoing. He pitched forward across the midships thwart and all consciousness left him.

IV

Charlotte

1

A physical impact at once cold and stinging was Honeyburn's first sensation when his senses returned. He made an inarticulate sound of protest and tried to raise himself from his recumbent position.

'Belay that!' said a cracked voice shrilly. 'Beg your pardon, sir,' added Mr Trapp severely, 'but you ain't condolescent yet by no manner o' means. You can sit up maybe, I say maybe, when I've got this 'ere bandage on, an' not before.'

Honeyburn relaxed again. He was lying on his back on the cot in his cabin, he perceived, and the carpenter was doing something to his leg. His knee hurt and he felt very weak.

'What's that stuff you're putting on my knee?' he demanded feebly.

'Biscay water,' returned Mr Trapp. 'Naught like good salt water for disaffectin' a wound, a deep 'un like you got. Lorst you a gallon o' blood, I shouldn't wonder. Got it tacklin' a French sojer bare-'anded and 'im with a bagnet, 'cordin' to what I 'ear Mr Fitzjames say. – 'Old taut, sir.'

Honeyburn winced as Mr Trapp began his bandaging; and with the wince recollection of the shore expedition flooded back to him. And of the return to the boat, and the rescued swimmer – a girl. The realisation that *Cracker* was under way, with (presumably) Fitzjames in charge, came now, belatedly.

'How long since I was brought on board?' he demanded.

'Not above twenty minutes, sir. You an' the mamzelle 'ad to be slung aboard with a yardarm tackle. Mr Fitzjames says to get sail on 'er –'

'That girl was brought on board, *here*? Good gr –' Honeyburn checked himself. 'She should have been put ashore. What in heaven's name are we to – Mr Trapp, please to go on deck and send Mr Fitzjames to me instantly.'

'Aye aye, sir.' The carpenter went on bandaging. 'The hinstant I got this 'ere made fast. 'Im what turns 'is 'and from the plough 'ad better 'ave a milestone round 'is neck, as the Bible says.'

Honeyburn's impatience was fast overcoming his weakness. Impotence and anxiety between them sharpened his tone.

'Where is this – this female now?'

Mr Trapp's wrinkled face cracked in a grin. 'In Mr Fitzjames's cabin, gettin' rigged in some of 'is duds. Come to 'er senses soon as we got 'er aboard and the two on 'em set to talkin' French and fixed that up, seemingly.' He tied-off the ends of the bandage and stood back to survey the effect. 'There y'are, sir, and King George's own surgeon couldn't do no better. You lie quiet for a spell and don't shift it –'

'I'll do nothing of the kind!' Honeyburn sat up gingerly. 'Get me into that chair by the table and send Mr Fitzjames to me.'

Mr Trapp opened his mouth to protest but a glance at his captain's face decided him against it.

'Aye, aye, sir,' he said, 'but don't blame me if we starts a hembridge.'

With some difficulty Honeyburn was got into the chair, where he sat with his bandaged leg stretched stiffly out and throbbing painfully. He was suddenly conscious of an intense thirst.

'Bring water,' he said curtly. 'There's a carafe in the locker.'

The carpenter fetched the carafe and with it a bottle. 'A

noggin' o' wine won't do you no 'arm neither,' he announced, eyeing his patient's drawn features. 'Wine, sir, is what we calls a restoratorive, apart from bein' a stimuliant –'

'Get Mr Fitzjames!' Honeyburn shouted at him.

'Aye aye, sir!' said Mr Trapp hastily, and departed.

Honeyburn emptied the water-carafe in two draughts and felt better. When he had poured some wine and drunk that also some of his irascibility faded and he regretted his brusque treatment of Mr Trapp. But exasperation remained. Here was *Cracker* under way, presumably on course for Orio, with a kidnapped Frenchwoman on board, and himself (he had reluctantly to admit it) unable to drag himself up to his quarterdeck; unless he risked some subterfuge such as smuggling the woman ashore at Orio he would have to report her presence to the naval authorities there, which meant that he would have to make the report he had resolved not to make. Was it too late to rectify Fitzjames's mistake? He could put the gun-brig about – she could hardly have made more than two miles from the coast – and return his unwanted passenger even now. But that might not be so easy. There was the possibility that the Frenchman he had killed had been discovered, the alarm given, armed men sent to the beach, perhaps with a field-piece –

There was a knock on the cabin door and Fitzjames came in. Honeyburn was aware at once of a change in his lieutenant. He was smiling, for one thing, and his face had lost the wooden sullenness that had been its invariable expression since he joined *Cracker*. But there was more to it than that, though Honeyburn couldn't lay a finger on it.

'Sir,' said Fitzjames, 'I'm happy to see you're on an even keel again. I hope –'

'Thank you, Mr Fitzjames,' Honeyburn cut him short, unsmiling. 'I await your report.'

'Yes, sir, of course. We're under main and tops'ls, course west by south pending your –'

'Your report concerning the unwarranted embarkation of an enemy national,' Honeyburn said sternly.

'An enemy – oh, I see.' Fitzjames's confidence collapsed into flustered embarrassment. 'Well, she insisted – she didn't want to be put ashore, sir. And there was you – I thought you'd better be got on board quick and your wound looked to. And she's a lady, sir, French aristocracy – though I didn't find that out until – but you'll want to speak with her yourself, no doubt,' he ended lamely.

'I certainly shall,' said Honeyburn grimly. 'However, I still require a proper report from you, Mr Fitzjames. You'll please to recount, and precisely, all that has happened since the moment when I – um – lost consciousness.'

Fitzjames visibly pulled himself together. 'Aye aye, sir. Well, after you swooned Gomez supported you on the stern thwart while Peters and I worked on the girl – we thought she was dead, drowned, at first. We put my coat on the midships thwart, laid her across it belly-down, and rocked her to empty the seawater out of her. 'Twas the best we could do, sir – a barrel would have been better.'

'Yes, yes, I know. You succeeded and she came to.'

'Yes, sir. I put my arm – I helped her to sit up and then Peters asks hadn't we better put about and take her back ashore. She heard that – she understands some English, sir – and called out, in French, that she'd rather drown than go back and that she wanted to be taken to England. So I ordered pull for the ship. There was your own condition to be thought of too, sir,' he added quickly.

'Just so,' Honeyburn said drily. 'But I understand from Mr Trapp that this young woman was hoisted on board unconscious.'

'She was, in a way – that is – I rather fancy, sir, that the unconsciousness was feigned.'

'Indeed!'

'Because the moment she was swung inboard and the triple-bowline taken off she stood up, sir, and did a sort of little dance.'

There was about Fitzjames's face, as he spoke these words, something of the expression of one who recalls a pleasant dream.

'In-deed!' said Honeyburn again, with more emphasis. 'And was this, may I ask, when the young person divulged that she was of noble blood?'

'No, sir,' Fitzjames said stiffly. 'That was later. But I should have said that we got you on board first and you were carried straight to your cabin. We got under away at once – main and tops'ls, course sou'-west by west. I've told Mr Grattan to cook a meal for you,' he added. 'I've had a mouthful myself.'

'Thank you,' Honeyburn said without sarcasm; he was beginning to realise the emptiness of his stomach.

'And I forgot to mention, sir, that this young lady is the one who came along the beach and spoke to Gomez and Peters while we were on the dunes.'

'I had guessed as much. Pray continue your report.'

'There's little more to tell, sir. I took mademoiselle at once to my cabin – the hands were staring and grinning – and told her to take off her wet things and get into anything of mine she could find. While she was doing this we talked –'

'Eh?' Honeyburn, forgetting his wound, sat back so suddenly that he hurt his leg abominably. 'You –'

'We talked through the closed door,' Fitzjames said somewhat loudly, reddening. 'She told me her name – Charlotte de Coulanges – and that she is seventeen years old. Her mother was the Comtesse de Coulanges. Her father and mother are both dead and she's been living at a château close to Labenne – that's the village we saw from the dunes, sir, and she says it's three leagues north of Bayonne. She hates Bonaparte and wants to get to England – saw her chance and risked her life on it. Sir –' he set his hands on the table and leaned across it earnestly – 'we must take her, sir!'

Honeyburn spared a moment to wonder at this urgency and at the new Fitzjames, so different from the sulky young oaf of his earlier acquaintance. He looked no older than a fifth-form schoolboy and his grey eyes pleaded like a spaniel's. His plea was nonsense, all the same.

'*Cracker* is not bound for England, Mr Fitzjames, as you well know,' he said, relaxing his severity a little. 'At Orio I may be ordered to remain on the Spanish coast or given some other duty. Moreover, it's out of the question for this Mademoiselle de Coulanges to sail for England in a King's ship with no other woman on board.' He checked Fitzjames's protest with a hand firmly raised. 'We shall defer this matter until I've spoken with mademoiselle, if you please.'

Overhead as he spoke the ship's bell sounded, two double clangs. Four bells of the afternoon watch, Honeyburn told himself; of a sudden he felt inexpressibly tired.

'Aye aye, sir,' Fitzjames said reluctantly. 'She may not be – er – ready to see you just yet,' he added hesitantly.

'Oh? Why not, pray?'

'Well, sir, I told her you'd want to see her soon as you'd recovered and she said she'd see no one until we'd found her a – a skirt, sir.'

'Good gracious!' Honeyburn concealed a grin. 'What does she think we are – a floating *couturière*'s? To the best of my knowledge we haven't a single item of feminine gear on board.'

'No, sir. But I spoke to Mr Sholto about it and he suggested a plan. There's an old Spanish ensign in the flag-locker and Timmis is sewing at it now. We had to guess at her waist-size of course, sir.'

'Of course,' nodded Honeyburn solemnly.

He considered for a moment. The urge to sleep and the need to eat were insistent, each striving for supremacy, and he would be forced to give way to one or both very soon. It was hot in the cabin and his mind moved sluggishly. There was no urgency about interviewing the French girl – she'd have to stay on board until Orio where he would put her ashore – but Fitzjames must be given orders for the course of the gun-brig.

'Bring the chart here, if you please,' he said.

With the chart spread on the table between them Honeyburn felt for the first time that he had the support and cooperation of a first lieutenant. It was Fitzjames who pointed out eagerly that since Bayonne and Cap Breton were both marked on the chart behind the coastline they could now, with the information provided by Charlotte de Coulanges, establish *Cracker*'s position with fair exactitude. Labenne was nine miles north of Bayonne and the gun-brig had therefore anchored off the coast five miles south of Cap Breton. Honeyburn used pencil and dividers and Fitzjames's estimate of her rate of knots to fix his present position and decided that he was now some 48 sea-miles from Orio. His best landfall of the Spanish coast, now that he was so far to eastward of his original course, was the projecting headland of Cape Higuier 20 miles east of Orio. He applied the protractor and looked up.

'I shall alter course south by west,' he told Fitzjames. 'That's the course for Cape Higuier, and we should make our landfall before sundown. I intend to heave-to for the night five miles off the coast and make sail at first light for Orio. Three hours' sail and we'll reach the port well inside the forenoon watch. Who has the deck?'

'It's my watch, sir, but Mr Sholto took over while I came below.'

'Very well. My compliments to Mr Sholto and he'll please to remain in charge of the deck from now until the end of the second dog-watch. Give him the new course and tell him you're to be called if a sail is sighted or the weather changes.' Weariness clogged his tongue and he had to force himself to speak the words with precision. 'You yourself will turn in – Mr Sholto will lend you his berth – and get as much sleep as you can.'

Fitzjames looked a protest but didn't utter it. 'Aye aye, sir. But – if I may suggest it, sir – it seems to me we could make Orio tonight. The wind's dropped to a five-knot breeze but it's still steady from the east, and if we got all sail on her –'

'No. I know nothing of Orio save that there's little there but an anchorage, and that anchorage will be crowded with shipping. Lord Wellington's supply vessels, transports, guard-ships – I'm not going to grope my way in by night, Mr Fitzjames.'

Twenty-four hours ago, Honeyburn realised suddenly, he wouldn't have thought of explaining his motives for such a decision to Fitzjames. The explanation had flowed easily on the current of new understanding between them and he found that peculiarly satisfying.

'See Band before you turn in,' he added, 'and tell him I want that hot meal brought to me. And a boathook, too, the short one from the cock-boat.'

'A – a boathook, sir?'

He had to smile at the young man's dropped jaw. 'I'll need a staff when I get under way again.'

'Oh – yes, sir, of course.' Fitzjames hesitated. 'And – Mademoiselle de Coulanges, sir?'

Honeyburn was tired of Mademoiselle de Coulanges.

'I'll see her in here at two bells of the second dog-watch,' he said shortly. 'See that I'm called then, if you please. Meanwhile she will remain in your cabin.'

'Aye aye, sir. But shouldn't we offer her some – er – refreshment?'

'See Mr Grattan and do what you think fit,' said Honeyburn.

He was so weary that he hardly noticed that Fitzjames had left the cabin until the lieutenant reopened the door and put his head in, to speak briefly and with embarrassed rapidity.

'Sir, I believe you saved my life this afternoon and I'm most grateful.'

He was gone without waiting for a reply. Honeyburn stared at the closed door and shook his head. That was nonsense, of course. The Frenchman had had to be silenced, and if he had thereby been prevented from using his bayonet on Fitzjames it was a secondary consideration. All the same, it was pleasant to have the boy's gratitude, pleasant too that he had discarded his silly mask of sullen indifference. But these were the only pleasant things in a prospect that held too many looming troubles: this French miss to be disposed of, the censure that awaited him at Orio when he made his report –

His descent into gloom was halted by the arrival of Shorty Band, juggling precariously with a steaming platter and a boathook. He told Band to put the boathook beside his cot and dismissed him without ceremony. Mr Grattan had done well. The beef was tender, the bread was not too stale, and there was a jug of gravy piping hot. Two mouthfuls and a sip of wine revived Honeyburn's spirits and he ate in a kind of comfortable dream. Whether or not by reason of Mr Trapp's ministrations his leg had ceased to pain him, and the events of the past twelve hours recurred hazily and at a great distance, as if they had happened years ago. That the shore adventure had been a piece of folly and a complete failure into the bargain seemed of little moment now; the hands that had wrung the life from a man among the Landes dunes must have belonged to someone else. Shorty Band, looking into the cabin ten minutes later, found his commanding officer sound asleep with his head on the table.

The carpenter and the cook had to be summoned to assist in getting Honeyburn into his cot and though he emitted a groan or two his eyes remained closed.

'There ain't no physic like the arms o' Morphuous,' said Mr Trapp, standing back to regard his patient with smug satisfaction. 'Give 'im five hours, five hours I say, and 'e'll be 'obblin' about as good as new. Unless,' he added thoughtfully, ''is luck's out and the wound takes bad. And there'll be no luck in this barky with a woman aboard.'

'Sure and there's one who doesn't think so,' said Mr Grattan. 'Young Cocky has his eyes on sticks for her.'

2

In the event, Honeyburn did not achieve Mr Trapp's prescribed five hours. He woke of his own accord, conscious first of a nagging pain in his knee and then of a worry that hung in his mind like the afterthought of a troublesome dream. By the pulsing rush of water along the hull and the tilt of the cabin deck he could tell that *Cracker* was on the port tack and making five or six knots. He discovered that a slight shift of his right leg removed nearly all the pain and lay for some moments collecting his thoughts and trying to locate the cause of that vague worry. Something left undone, some precaution neglected in fatigue before sleep overtook him? Something to do with the chart. He had laid a course for Cape Higuier as being the nearest landfall; and he had done that with the single eye of a seaman for coastline and soundings, ignoring in his overspent state the factor of war.

He had been laid on his cot fully clothed and his watch was in his pocket: it was six o'clock. Four hours' sleep had marvellously restored his mental alertness and he groped for and found the staff which Shorty Band had hooked onto the cot, aware that a cool damp air was seeping into the cabin. The anticipated stab of pain when he swung his legs to the deck and stood up didn't come. Supporting himself with the boathook, he found he could walk, albeit stiffly; the wound had undoubtedly been no more than a flesh-wound and if the tightness of Mr Trapp's bandaging could be trusted cautious movement wouldn't reopen it.

He took the chart from the rack and spread it on the table. There was Cape Higuier – it must be only a few leagues south of *Cracker* now – in enemy territory, sixteen miles or so east of San Sebastian where Wellington was struggling to break the French defence and open the way into France. The three-mile-long promontory was flanked on the east by a deep and wide bay with the name *Fuenterrabia* at its inner end. Doubtless the French had fortifications there and elsewhere to defend the coast against a possible landing to take them in rear, and they would have a battery on the cape itself; but they could have no armed vessels of any force in this corner of the Bay or they would have been heard of before now.

Honeyburn told himself that while he had been negligent in omitting earlier consideration of this he had no cause to worry. All he needed was a sight of the cape, and for that there was no need to come within range of the probable fort or battery. He was rolling up the chart when Fitzjames entered the cabin and halted in some surprise.

'I beg your pardon, sir,' he began. 'I thought you'd still be –'

'I'm sufficiently recovered, Mr Fitzjames. What is it? Have we sighted Cape Higuier?'

'No, sir, Mr Sholto called me and I considered you should be told. The weather's changed – wind's veered a point to southward and we're into a sea-mist – puffs of it, sir, clearing every few minutes and then closing in again. We've lookouts at fore and main and by Mr Sholto's reckoning we're eight or nine miles off the coast.'

Honeyburn considered, frowning. The sea-mist was a nuisance but he needed that landfall and there should be the certainty of it in a clearance. The coast was not a lee shore – even less so with the wind veering south – and the danger was negligible if he approached cautiously.

'What sail we are carrying?' he demanded.

'Courses and tops'ls only, sir.'

'I'll have the courses taken in, if you please. Take a bearing of the cape as soon as it's sighted and then bear away nor'west.' He shifted his leg impatiently, half minded to have himself carried on deck; at a pinch, he thought, he could even manage it by himself. 'You'll report to me, of course.'

'Yes, sir.' Fitzjames hesitated a second. 'It's half-an-hour short of two bells, when you said you'd see Mademoiselle de Coulanges, but perhaps –'

'Good gracious!' Honeyburn had actually forgotten all about his unwelcome passenger. 'I'd better – yes, Mr Fitzjames. Please to bring her here at once.'

Fitzjames's 'aye aye, sir' came over his shoulder as he spun round and sprang up the ladder. Honeyburn settled himself in his chair at the table with his leg stretched stiffly out and tried hurriedly to get himself into the proper mood for talking in French; he was of those who find it easier to understand the spoken language than to speak it. From on deck came Fitzjames's voice shouting orders and he felt the list and swing as *Cracker* altered course. Should he get his lieutenant to help him with this interview? He dismissed the idea at once – Fitzjames, already the girl's champion, would be a nuisance. The girl was nuisance enough but he would have to show her due courtesy. He should have had a chair placed for her –

'Mademoiselle de Coulanges, sir,' said Fitzjames, entering with his charge. '*J'ai l'honneur de* –' He broke off, apparently deciding that French formalities were out of place. 'This is Captain Honeyburn, mademoiselle.'

Honeyburn found himself staring at what seemed to be a child dressed for a Yuletide masquerade. She was not much more than five feet tall, though the fair hair piled high on her head (and tied with a piece of spunyarn) made her look taller. One of Fitzjames's shirts hung in loose folds from her shoulders and from the waist downwards she was enveloped in the gaudy red-and-yellow of a Spanish ensign.

'*Monsieur le capitaine*,' she murmured, dropping a not ungraceful curtsey.

'*Mademoiselle*,' said Honeyburn, inclining his head; he cleared his throat.'*Pardonnez-moi que je reste assis, je vous en prie*.'

'*Je comprends parfaitement, monsieur*,' she said, looking up at him with quick sympathy. '*Georges m'a dit – vous êtes blessé*.'

Who the deuce was Georges? Of course – Fitzjames. These youngsters had wasted no time on convention.

'Thank you, Mr Fitzjames,' he said dismissively. 'See that

I'm informed when Cape Higuier is sighted. *Asseyez-vous, mademoiselle,*' he went on as Fitzjames departed with evident reluctance. '*Apportez, s'il vous plaît, la chaise là-bas.*'

The girl brought the chair to the table and seated herself facing him. She had hazel eyes and a small slightly tip-tilted nose, and her face, evenly tanned to a pale biscuit colour, had an odd elfin charm. Honeyburn's taste was for more shape in a woman (Cecilia Tuftoe had a very comfortable figure) and Charlotte de Coulanges was slim to the point of skinniness. He had been considering her for several seconds without speaking and Charlotte evidently mistook his silence for a lack of vocabulary.

'*Je ne parle pas bien anglais,*' she ventured with a faint smile, '*mais* –' She produced a slow-spoken sentence. 'One says – that the Captain Honeyburn he has – the kind heart and will travel me to England.'

Honeyburn could not repress a smile but quickly twisted his features into severity. With his first sentences safely out he felt more confident of his ability to converse.

'We shall speak in French, mademoiselle, if you please,' he said in that language. 'And I must tell you first that I am not going to England but to Orio in Spain. Secondly, it is not – um – proper for a lady of birth to journey unaccompanied in a vessel with forty-five men.'

'But, monsieur –'

'At Orio we shall discuss what is to be done. Meanwhile, mademoiselle, you will please to tell me, with exactitude, how and why you came to be swimming in the sea this morning. Mr Fitzjames has informed me that you are –' the word for 'orphan' eluded Honeyburn and he changed his phrase – 'that your parents are both dead and that you have been living in the château near Labenne. Is that correct?'

For a moment the girl looked as though she was going to ignore his questions and renew her entreaties; but a glance at Honeyburn's rigid countenance dissuaded her and after a brief pause to collect herself she spoke calmly and clearly.

'It is true, monsieur. My father the Comte de Coulanges

was killed when I was two years old, fighting in the Austrian army against Bonaparte. My mother the Comtesse died five years later. I have no brothers or sisters and I was taken into the care of the Sisters of Saint Catherine at Toulouse. Then, a year ago when I was sixteen, I came to live at the Château Labenne with Madame Cazalet, an old friend of my mother –'

She spoke more quickly as she went on and Honeyburn had once to interrupt with a '*plus lentement, s'il vous plaît*', but he followed her story without difficulty. For a long time, she said, she had longed to escape from a country ruled over by the tyrant Bonaparte who had killed her father; to escape to England whither her mother's sister Madame de Goursac had fled in the early years of the Revolution. There had been no chance of this until sudden opportunity had offered itself that morning. With the coming of the hot weather Charlotte had persuaded Madame Cazalet to allow her to bathe in the sea each morning, accompanied by Berthe the fat housekeeper. Today they had seen the ship anchored off the beach and the boat with the two men on the beach, had spoken to the men and been answered in Spanish. Charlotte had known that they were English though she had not told Berthe this.

'How did you know, mademoiselle?' Honeyburn interrupted at this point.

She smiled suddenly at him, an impish and charming smile. 'There was a package under the seat at the back of the boat, monsieur, with English words painted in white paint.' She pronounced them, quaintly. ' "Bo-at's bag".'

Honeyburn grunted, annoyed with himself for forgetting that obvious announcement of nationality. All three of *Cracker*'s boats had a boat's bag, with its Admiralty-ordained contents of spunyarn and tallow and a dozen other useful items; cutter and longboat carried a seaboat's box as well, containing such things as lantern and axe and provisions. One of the things he had done while the gun-brig was in Portsmouth harbour was to check their contents and have bags and boxes clearly labelled.

'So then I knew,' Charlotte was saying, 'that the ship was an English ship. But I could not ask the men to take me to her – and there was Berthe, who must not know what I intended.'

The boat must be waiting for someone, she thought. She had undressed in the bathing-machine and attired herself for swimming, watched through a crack in the wooden side until she saw men coming down the beach to the boat, and then had launched herself from the machine hoping to intercept the boat's course.

'*Je suis bonne nageuse mais ça – c'était trop loin*,' she said feelingly. '*N'eût été Georges je suis noyé*.'

That Fitzjames had saved her from drowning was true enough and certainly not to be regretted; nevertheless, Honeyburn told himself, it would have saved a deal of present and future trouble if she hadn't given him the chance of doing it.

'It was then your carriage, mademoiselle, that was standing near the dunes,' he said.

'Madame Cazalet's carriage,' she amended. 'She has been kind to me – and yet I cannot love her. She permits me the carriage from the château to the beach, which is scarcely half-a-league, but forbade me when I wished to drive to Cap Breton to see the canal they are making there. And that is less than two leagues. Now, indeed, the road has been closed by the military.'

At mention of Cap Breton Honeyburn, who had been rubbing his chin and wondering what he should do with her, stiffened and leaned suddenly across the table. The action hurt his knee but he hardly noticed it.

'Cap Breton? A canal there?' he said sharply. 'Why are they doing this, mademoiselle?'

Charlotte looked surprised at his urgency. '*Je ne sais pas, monsieur*.' She shrugged. 'In Labenne it is said they have joined the lake to the harbour. At Cap Breton there is a very, very small harbour, you understand.'

'And the lake – what lake is this?'

'A long narrow lake, monsieur. The people here call them *étangs*, and this one is the Étang d'Hossegor. The end nearest Cap Breton is only a very little way from the harbour.' The hazel eyes regarded him cautiously. 'Was it something to do with the new canal, monsieur, that caused you to land from your ship and go into the dunes?'

Honeyburn ignored the question. Excitement was rising in him. Here at last was a fact to support McCormick's flimsy theory – new and very recent activity at Cap Breton. How the digging of a canal could threaten Wellington's supply ships he didn't yet see but there must surely be some connection.

'Mademoiselle,' he said earnestly, 'I beg you will answer some questions I shall ask.' He paused, frowning. 'You are a Frenchwoman and I am an enemy of France. If you prefer not to answer –'

'It is the France of Bonaparte you fight against!' she broke in hotly; the hazel eyes were flashing now. 'To bring down the Corsican is to free the world – I would fight him myself if I could! Ask your questions, monsieur.'

Honeyburn's heart warmed towards her. Cecilia Tuftoe had expressed the same sentiment in much the same words at their last meeting; but while he found it difficult to picture Mrs Tuftoe handling sword or musket effectively it was easy to imagine Charlotte doing so.

'Tell me when this canal-digging began,' he said.

The girl reflected. 'I think it must have been at the beginning of July, not before. Because only then could the heavy wagons travel on the road.'

'Heavy wagons – on the road to Cap Breton? What did they carry, mademoiselle?'

'Monsieur, I can tell you only what I have heard from Berthe. Château Labenne, you must understand, is not on the road but stands apart from the village. Berthe goes to Labenne to make purchases and gossip and I learned of these wagons from her.' She regarded him inquiringly. 'Are they, then, of so much importance?'

Honeyburn was not prepared to admit a French national, however Royalist her sympathies, to his inconclusive theories. He restrained his growing excitement and made himself speak less eagerly.

'They could be of no importance, mademoiselle. But if you would tell me all you know about them, or have heard, you would greatly oblige me.'

Charlotte nodded and wrinkled her brow in an effort of recollection. It was at the end of June, she said, when men had come from Bayonne to repair the road, which had then been little more than a rough track for farm carts. A week or ten days had passed and then a great many wagons had passed through Labenne, coming from Bayonne three leagues away. Some had carried men, Berthe had told her, but most were laden with timber, wooden boards, she thought. One of the drivers had told a villager that they were going to Cap Breton to build wooden sheds for the canal-diggers. Two days later the wagons had returned unladen and quite a long time afterwards – at the end of last month, it was – more wagons had gone through Labenne on their way north, but that had been in the night. Only one man, awakened by the rumble of wheels, had looked from his window and seen them, and he had told Berthe that there were twelve big wagons each drawn by six horses. He could see nothing of their loads, but it was evident that they were very heavy.

Guns? Honeyburn felt increasingly confident that he was hot on the trail of something here.

'And it was after these wagons had gone to Cap Breton that the road was closed by the military?' he asked.

'Ah, but this was another matter,' Charlotte said. 'Three weeks ago a notice was posted in the village – one of Bonaparte's departmental orders. It said that the region between Labenne and Cap Breton was declared a military training area for army conscripts and that no one could travel on the road without a special permit. We should have been grateful to the Emperor, I suppose,' she added with youthful sarcasm, 'that we were allowed to use the track to the beach.'

Honeyburn was sitting with his bony fingers spread on the table and his frowning gaze fixed unseeing on his fingers. His mind was busy with dates and possibilities. June 21st – that was the day of Vitoria, the battle that resulted in the defeat of one French army and the retreat of another. After Vitoria it must have been plain to Bonaparte, or whoever commanded in his absence, that Wellington was going to throw all his strength into achieving the invasion of France by way of the western passes of the Pyrenees, between the mountains and the Bay. The British army owed its successes to the British command of the sea, to the supply-line from England which moved its terminus eastward from port to port to keep pace with the army's advance. And as the French retreated, as the decisive battle for the frontier drew nearer, that supply-line was moving nearer and nearer to the Landes coast. Surely, Honeyburn thought, the minds of the French command would move along the lines McCormick had suggested and a plan for attacking the convoy route would be swiftly devised and put into operation. He himself was now almost certain that it had.

For the dates Charlotte had given him fell neatly into place; too neatly to be coincidental. Less than ten days after Vitoria the road to Cap Breton from Bayonne had been repaired to bear heavy vehicles; a week later 'a great many wagons' (he wished he knew how many) had taken men and material to Cap Breton; about three weeks after that the twelve big wagons, heavy six-horse drays probably, had gone there. It all fitted with the hypothesis that some kind of warship was being constructed – had been constructed, by now – at Cap Breton for the destruction of the British convoys. That some attempt to keep it secret had been made seemed clear; the conscript training area, the eventual closure of the road, pointed to that. As for the digging of the canal from the Hossegor lake, that might have something to do with the plan or could be a deception, an excuse to cover the arrival of a ship's company at Cap Breton. In such matters the French were notable for taking precautions against possible spies. Honeyburn remembered the convoy sailing-date being bandied about in the Portsmouth tavern; that wouldn't happen in Bonaparte's France. And, come to think of it, that convoy –

'*S'il vous plaît, monsieur le capitaine* –'

Charlotte's voice, low and hesitant, made him suddenly aware that he had been sitting silent and motionless for several minutes.

'I ask pardon, mademoiselle,' he said hastily. 'My thoughts engaged me.'

'Do not think me shameless, monsieur, if I ask whether your thoughts concerned Charlotte de Coulanges.'

She looked extremely appealing and Honeyburn felt a touch of remorse. It was true that she had got herself on board his ship unasked and unwanted, without clothes or money, to saddle him with an awkward problem. But the information she had given him had relieved another awkward problem by making his unauthorised shore excursion productive of valuable evidence. And in subjecting her to a prolonged questioning he had forgotten that the girl must be intensely anxious to know what was to be done with her.

'Listen now, mademoiselle,' he said in a kinder tone than he had hitherto used. 'Tomorrow this ship will arrive in Orio, where there will be other British vessels. It will not be possible for you to –'

He stopped in mid-sentence, arrested by a succession of sounds from the deck: the screech of the masthead lookout, Fitzjames's bellow, the boatswain's voice shouting orders and the thudding of hurrying feet. Hard on the heels of these noises came a clatter on the companion-ladder and Fitzjames appeared in the cabin doorway.

'By'r leave, sir,' he said a trifle breathlessly, 'we've just sighted Cape Higuier through a gap in the mist. It's a scant mile away, sir – and abaft the starboard beam!' The deck tilted as he spoke. 'I've ordered her put about, sir –'

'Get me on deck!' snapped Honeyburn, heaving himself up from his chair; and, as both Fitzjames and the girl began to protest, 'Give me that boathook and help me up the ladder – lively, now!'

Somehow, between lifting and pushing, they got him on deck and leaning against the port rail just for'ard of the quarterdeck, where he steadied himself with the boathook and swept a rapid glance all round him. It was a curious seascape that met his gaze. On every hand alleyways of rippled water reached into the filmy coils of the sea-mist that crawled across the surface, its slow movement continually opening long vistas of sea only to close them again. The upper vapours of the mist were tinted saffron-colour by the light of the sinking sun. There was no land in sight anywhere that Honeyburn could see.

Cracker was in process of going about, very slowly because she wore so little canvas, and wherever Cape Higuier was it wasn't abaft the starboard beam now. Fitzjames had dashed to the binnacle and was stooping over the compass. As the gun-brig completed her turn and steadied on the opposite course he straightened himself and gazed intently into the mist on the port hand. His call came in a few seconds.

'There, sir – there!'

Honeyburn had no need of his pointing hand. A rift had opened in the mist, to show a vignette of a green headland with low cliffs flanking it and a line of white water at their base. It was hardly more than half-a-mile away, and *Cracker*, with the south-easterly breeze over her quarter, was creeping slowly out past the headland to bring it on her beam. It was so close that he could make out the embrasures in the wall that fronted the low stone building on the end of the cape, and see men moving by the wall.

'Mr Sholto! he yelled at the top of his voice. 'Pipe all hands. Mr Fitzjames, get all sail on her. Starboard helm,

Driscoll – hold her there.'

Was this last the right decision? *Cracker* was heading away from the cape now, opening the range, but the rift in the mist was widening rather than closing and a broad stretch of open water lay ahead. While Sholto's whistle shrilled and the hands raced aloft Honeyburn's jostling thoughts dwelt for a moment on what had happened – some unpredictable current setting the gun-brig to eastward of her course for Cape Higuier so that in the sea-mist she had stood in past the invisible headland into the bay of Fuenterrabia. And it was no mere battery on the cape but a fort, and *Cracker* was well within range if, as was probable, they had 32-pounders up there. Now, though, she was beginning to surge ahead as the sails were let fall and sheeted home; a vessel moving at seven or eight knots was a difficult target. On the other hand, none knew better than he the vast improvement in accuracy when a gun was fired from a perfectly stable emplacement instead of the shifting deck of a ship.

Someone touched his arm. 'Monsieur –'

He turned to find that Charlotte and Mr Trapp had carried up a chair from the cabin and set it against the rail. He thanked them and lowered himself into it, though his knee had been giving no pain.

'By rights you did ought to be layin' quiet, sir,' Mr Trapp said severely. 'I'll want to take a look at that there bandage –'

'*Voilà*!' cried Charlotte, pointing ahead.

Honeyburn had been watching the fort and had seen the flash, but he turned his head quickly enough to see the white fountain raised by the fall of shot thirty fathoms ahead. Over – but dead in line. The heavy *boom*! was certainly the report of a 32-pounder. The rolling mist showed no sign of closing the rift but it lay thickly away on his port bow.

'Port a point,' he told Driscoll, and on the words a column of water rose like a tall water-sprite a biscuit-toss out from the rail.

They had two guns firing now and no doubt they'd have more in action in five minutes, but five minutes was all

Cracker needed to gain the cover of the sea-mist – providing the mist didn't change its present formation or lift altogether. Another shot, and another one three seconds after it. He failed to observe their fall but Fitzjames called to him from his stance farther for'ard.

'Port bow, sir, both ahead and close together, six fathoms clear.'

Whoever was in charge of those guns knew his business. And one hit on the waterline from a 32-pounder ball could sink the gun-brig. Three flashes in quick succession from the fort. As the third caught his eyes Honeyburn received a cold douche across head and shoulders – the splash raised by a ball close under *Cracker*'s quarter.

'*Ah, c'est affreux*!' cried Charlotte ecstatically, her eyes shining with excitement.

It crossed Honeyburn's mind, belatedly, that he ought to have sent her to her cabin as soon as the firing began. It hardly mattered now, however, for headland and fort were fading from sight behind a thickening veil of mist. In a few seconds they had vanished altogether and *Cracker* was sailing into maze of billowing clouds whose upper vapours were aglow with the orange hues of sunset.

Honeyburn had been unaware that he was holding his breath. He let it out now in a sigh of relief. It would be as well, he thought, to hold on, get well into the cover of the mist, and then make a sharp alteration of course. As he reached this decision there was a mighty crash for'ard and the gun-brig lurched over to starboard so suddenly that he had to clutch the rail to save his chair from sliding. A double *boom*! from the unseen fort, a chorus of yells from the men on the foredeck, and he saw the foremast with its fluttering upper sails topple and fall, shot clean through below the topmast crosstrees.

3

Recollecting that moment some time afterwards, Honeyburn was to remember that his first emotion was a burning resentment. It was unjust, unfair, that the French gunners should bring off a lucky shot (nine-tenths lucky, at any rate) when *Cracker* had won her escape. But it was no time to indulge emotions and his mind worked at feverish speed to sort commands into their proper order.

'The wheel, Fitzjames – help Driscoll. Mr Sholto! Take in all sail to the main course. Mr Trapp –' the carpenter had already started to go for'ard – 'see if you can free her from all that hamper. Let it go by the board.'

The unseen guns boomed again, and yet again, while he was speaking. His first need was to take his ship out of range. The fallen mast in its cocoon of tangled rigging had dropped across the starboard bow rail with its upper sails dragging in the water, aiding the gun-brig's natural tendency to fly up into the wind, and the utmost efforts of Driscoll and Fitzjames were hardly sufficient to hold her. Charlotte sprang unbidden from beside Honeyburn to clutch at the wheel-spokes in an attempt to help them. The movement dislodged the fastening of her makeshift skirt and it was too evident that she wore nothing beneath it.

'Peters!' yelled Honeyburn; the big seaman, who had just jumped down from the mainmast shrouds, came running.

'Lend Driscoll a hand at the wheel. Mr Fitzjames, take charge for'ard. Get storm and flying jibs on her – hoist all possible canvas. Then see that wreckage cut clear as soon as you can.'

'Aye aye, sir' came from halfway along the deck as Fitzjames leaped to obey.

Charlotte, hastily knotting the Spanish flag about her waist, returned as Honeyburn was trying to get on his feet.

'Give me a hand, my dear, if you please,' he said.

He had spoken in English but she understood him and helped him to stand up. Now he could look freely round him. The fort hadn't fired since those last two shots and the mist still hid them from it, but a rift might open at any moment and expose them to further bombardment. The last topmen came sliding down from the yards and *Cracker*'s mainmast was bare of sail save for the main course, making the task of the men at the helm very much easier. Up for'ard a swarm of men worked with axe and knife while the two jibs rose and filled on the bowsprit. He could see Fitzjames wielding an axe, hewing like a madman at some obstruction. A burst of cheering and the ruin of the foremast slipped free, to drift slowly past the gun-brig's side and vanish astern.

'Starboard helm. Steer due north.'

She turned very slowly, and before she had steadied on the new course the fort opened fire again, two shots in quick succession. Looking astern, Honeyburn saw the building and the top of the headland glowing ruby-red just above the upper tendrils of sunset-tinted mist that rose like flames around it. The splash of a third shot caught his eye; short by a good fifty fathoms. Under her low canvas *Cracker* seemed scarcely to be moving though she must be making three or four knots. But now she was nearly two miles away from Cape Higuier, and when the French gunners tried another shot – their last – he could see nothing of its fall. Five minutes later the gun-brig crept out from the mist onto the clear surface of a darkening sea, with the western horizon black against the splendour of red and gold left by the vanished sun and the Spanish coast invisible behind the low-lying bank of cloud.

The passing of the sun brought a chill to the air and the south-westerly breeze had freshened. Charlotte, who appeared to have constituted herself Honeyburn's attendant, fetched his boat-cloak from the cabin and assisted him to sit down again. Observing that she herself was shivering (the Spanish flag was old and threadbare) he suggested that she should retire to Fitzjames's cabin, and as she turned to obey the lieutenant came hurrying aft. Honeyburn noted the quick exchange of smiles, the brief and surreptitious touching of hands, before Charlotte went below and Fitzjames made his report.

'Nobody injured, sir. The lookout – Erikson, it was – hung on somehow when the mast fell and climbed inboard none the worse. The rail's a bloody – I mean a terrible mess, sir, between the two for'ard gunports starboard side. Mr Trapp's at work now closing the gap with scantling. He asked me to tell you that his repair isn't to be considered "pernament".'

They exchanged smiles; though not long ago Honeyburn would have resented the mild poking of fun at his carpenter.

'Very well,' he said. 'And the state of the foremast?'

'That was a damned unlucky shot, sir. We can carry the forecourse, naturally, but the Frogs have left us no more than a fathom and a half of mast above that. Mr Sholto reckons he can contrive to rig a scrap of canvas to do duty as a tops'l but it'll be a mere pocket-handkerchief.'

Honeyburn frowned, reflecting. It was impossible that he could obtain, or ship, a new mast in Orio; impossible, moreover, that a vessel crippled as *Cracker* now was could be employed in operations on the Spanish coast. She would certainly be sent straight home to refit, and with her sail area drastically reduced the homeward voyage would be a long one.

'My compliments to Mr Sholto,' he said, 'and he is to take what steps he thinks fit to ensure we can hoist a second sail on what's left of the foremast. – Wait,' he added as Fitzjames began to move. 'Tell him I intend to heave-to for the night six miles off the coast. When that's done he may pipe hands to supper. And Mr Fitzjames, I shall be happy if you will sup with me in my cabin. Perhaps –'

He stopped himself on the brink of suggesting that Mademoiselle de Coulanges might join them for supper. It would never do for a young woman attired only in a shirt and a thin Spanish flag to sup with two naval officers, one of them young and impressionable.

'Perhaps you'll see Mr Grattan and arrange for a meal to be taken to your cabin for Mademoiselle de Coulanges,' he amended. 'And I believe we may send her a glass of Bordeaux as well. If mademoiselle has never been under fire before she behaved remarkably well.'

'Yes, sir – thank you, sir!' said Fitzjames with great enthusiasm. 'Did you notice, sir, how damned quick she was, jumping to help when we couldn't get the wheel over?'

'She was certainly quick.'

'If she sailed with us to England,' Fitzjames went on in a rush, 'she could be of some use, sir. Help Grattan, maybe even tail onto a halyard –'

'It won't do,' Honeyburn cut in firmly. 'You may set your mind at rest, however. I shall make it my business to see that mademoiselle reaches England in due course and with company of her own sex. Meanwhile I shall arrange for some respectable female at Orio to take charge of her. She is a Catholic, of course, and conceivably there are nuns at Orio. Now carry on, if you please.'

Fitzjames departed looking downcast and Mr Trapp, passing him, came aft to report his repair of the shattered bulwarks completed.

'Temperry it 'as to be,' he ended, 'but it'll stand up till we gets some better timber for it.'

'If it stands up as well as your work on my knee it will do excellently,' said Honeyburn; perhaps in reaction after the past half-hour of tension, he felt exhilarated. 'Observe.' With the aid of the boathook he hoisted himself to his feet. 'I shall be able to walk ashore at Orio, Mr Trapp.'

He cut short the carpenter's protests, which dwelt on the possibility of a hembridge, by requesting him to find Gomez and send him aft. The light was fast dying from the western sky and in the east a star was already winking. When Gomez came loping aft his long Spanish features (so oddly at variance with his cockney tongue) were scarcely distinguishable in the twilight.

'Mr Sholto's dooty, sir,' said Gomez, 'and we can 'eave-to whenever you gives the word.'

'Very well. When I go ashore tomorrow, Gomez, you'll come with me. Sunday rig. Take this chair down to my cabin and then tell Mr Sholto, with my compliments, that I shall heave-to in five minutes' time.'

It would be useful to have a Spanish-speaking seaman with him. Some kind of makeshift naval base must have been established in Orio and he would have to ask his way to it. Honeyburn gazed southward across the dark water to where the Spanish coast, still an enemy coast for fifteen miles west of the French frontier, lay hidden below the barely discernible horizon. *Cracker* was a good six miles out now, the wind was light and steady from the south-east and the weather appeared settled.

'Mr Fitzjames! We'll heave-to, if you please. – Bring her to the wind, Driscoll.'

The gun-brig turned slowly to starboard and lay with her unevenly-balanced canvas flapping. He watched without interfering while the boatswain and his men trotted back and forth adjusting sheets and braces and was glad to see that Fitzjames confined himself to overseeing the taking of a double reef in the maincourse; this was something that Sholto could do better than either of them. But the last of his ill-timed exhilaration fell from him as he surveyed poor *Cracker*'s stump of a foremast and untidy rig, and sudden recollection of the day's events made him shiver and pull his boat-cloak closer round him. In twenty-four hours he had contrived to get himself wounded in a hare-brained shore adventure, to make an error of navigation that had taken him dangerously close to the enemy coast, and to get his ship dismasted. It was a good thing, he reflected gloomily, that he had the news of French activity at Cap Breton to set against it; it would have been better if he could have been more precise about the nature of that activity.

Fitzjames and Sholto came aft and Honeyburn managed to forget his doubts in arranging the night's routine. The usual sea-watches would be kept; lookouts at bow and stern, no lights to be shown; Mr Sholto to take the first watch and Mr Fitzjames the middle watch. He himself, Honeyburn told them, was to be called for the morning watch and at first light they would make sail for Orio. He dispatched Fitzjames to see about their meal and accepted the boatswain's assistance in getting himself down to his cabin.

'She'll lie-to pretty comfortable if the weather don't change,' Sholto said as Honeyburn settled his bandaged leg under the table. 'But God help us, sir,' he added, 'if we fall in with one of them privateers before we're back in Portsmouth.'

Honeyburn said an inward *Amen*. 'Hands to supper, if you please, Mr Sholto,' he said aloud, 'and I fancy the circumstances warrant splicing the mainbrace.'

Ten minutes later, with the light of the slowly-swinging cabin lamp gleaming in shifting reflection from cutlery and bottle and glasses, he was awaiting the arrival of Fitzjames with some impatience. A delicious smell was drifting aft from the galley – Grattan must have roasted one of the dozen chickens they had taken on board at Porstmouth – and Hezekiah Band would be bringing the meal at any moment. Aboard *Cracker* the captain's meals had to be carried along the deck, and roast chicken should be served piping hot. In the event, the chicken and Fitzjames arrived simultaneously, the latter breathless and apologetic.

'I thought it as well to see that Charl – that mademoiselle had all that she wanted for the night, sir,' he explained.

'Very right and proper,' Honeyburn said drily. 'Please to sit down, Mr Fitzjames.'

He lifted the cover, dismissed his steward, and began to carve; he found himself extremely hungry.

'She detained me with some questions,' Fitzjames went on, sitting down at the table, 'about our purpose in landing last night. I told her I wasn't able to answer them.'

'Again, very right.' Honeyburn poured wine into the glasses and raised his own. '*Bon appetit*, Mr Fitzjames.'

'Thank you, sir,' said Fitzjames, taking a sip and setting down his glass. 'And she also told me of your own questions and the information she was able to give. It gave me an idea, sir, and I fancy I'm –'

'Shall we eat first and discuss your idea afterwards? Grattan's chicken deserves our full attention.'

They ate in silence for a minute or two before Honeyburn, the edge of his hunger blunted, remembered his duties as host and senior officer.

'No doubt Captain Decies dined his young gentlemen of the gunroom from time to time,' he said, abandoning knife and fork in favour of fingers for a chicken-leg. 'That would have been much more of a grand occasion than this.'

'Silver plate and hold your tongue till you're spoken to,' replied Fitzjames succinctly. 'I detested it. And Captain Decies knew who was my father. I suppose,' he added bitterly, 'I should have been grateful to him for inviting a bastard to his table.'

'If you'll allow me to say so,' Honeyburn said gently, 'I think you make too much of that.'

Fitzjames disregarded him. 'Captain Decies had a way of reminding me of it – a word or a look that no one else at the table would understand. I think he liked watching men squirm. And –' He stopped himself and looked at Honeyburn with a wry smile. 'And this is telling tales out of school, sir. I'll just add that there was no roast chicken as good as this aboard *Centaur* – and that I'm most happy to be serving in *Cracker*.'

'You were not always so, I fancy.'

'No,' Fitzjames admitted. 'I was newly promoted, you see, and *Centaur*'s lower-deck complement is six hundred – six hundred men at the bidding of George Fitzjames!' He wagged his head sagely. 'I doubt I was something of a young fool, sir. I resented being transferred to a gun-brig and being chevvied about by Mr Bloody Etheridge. I didn't know *Cracker* then. And if I hadn't joined *Cracker* I'd never have met –' Here he appeared to be overtaken by a fit of coughing and took a drink of wine. 'But speaking of *Cracker*, I know little of her history, sir, except that she engaged and sank an American privateer in June. Was it a long engagement?'

Honeyburn, who had almost disposed of his platter of chicken, was not unwilling to recount the events of that successful action. Lieutenant Michael Fitton's skilful handling of his vessel in the crucial minutes lost nothing in the telling, though Honeyburn was emphatic in pointing out that it was accurate long-range gunnery that had made those manoeuvres possible. By the time the chicken bones were laid on one side and they were ending the meal with some passable Cheddar washed down with the last of the wine, he had passed on to the gun-brig's adventures in the Baltic a year ago.

'The Baltic timber convoys were vitally important to the Navy at that time,' he was saying, 'and the Danes knew it. On our first voyage we were attacked off Saltholm by four gunboats –'

'Gunboats!' exclaimed Fitzjames, setting his glass down with a sharp tap. 'I beg your pardon, sir, but this chimes with something I have in mind.'

'The idea you mentioned?' Honeyburn looked sharply at him. 'Mr Fitzjames, I believe I know what it is. But before we go further – allow me.' He distributed the last drops of the wine between their glasses and raised his own. 'The King, God bless him!'

It was the fashion nowadays, he knew, to add 'and His Royal Highness the Prince Regent', but he doubted whether his lieutenant would drink that toast. They drank it sitting, in naval style, and Honeyburn as he put down his glass added a quotation.

'*Moribus antiquis res stat*,' he said; and as Fitzjames raised puzzled eyebrows, 'which may be construed "the State is upheld by the observance of traditional custom." And that, let me reassure you, is my first and last essay in combining my naval duties with those of a schoolmaster.'

'Thank you, sir,' Fitzjames said gravely.

They exchanged grins and Honeyburn, warmed by a new sense of companionship, settled his stiff knee more comfortably and sat back in his chair.

'And now for this idea of yours,' he said.

'Yes, sir. First, though –' Fitzjames hesitated. 'You'll recall, perhaps, that you didn't tell me much about the rumour of French activities at Cap Breton.'

'At the time, Mr Fitzjames, your – um – manner did not invite confidences.'

'I know, sir, and I'm sorry for it.'

'Well, here is all I know of the matter,' said Honeyburn.

He told briefly of his conversation with McCormick of the *Crane*, his own speculations, and his resolve to take advantage of *Cracker*'s fast passage and try to see for himself.

'And I verily believe you've given me the solution to the problem,' he ended. 'In one word, gunboats.'

'That's it, depend upon it!' Fitzjames leaned eagerly across the table. 'It all fits perfectly – and if you think about it there's nothing else they could use.'

'To attack a convoy escorted by an eighteen-gun brig-sloop? To be certain of destroying it? And – what's more – to do this nine leagues off the coast? For the convoys for Orio will pass not far short of thirty sea-miles off Cap Breton.'

'A dozen gunboats could do it.' Fitzjames poked a finger at him. 'You're thinking, of course, of the gunboats that attacked you in the Baltic. How were they armed, sir?'

'Twelve-pounders, and ten men at the oars.'

'Ah – you were never in the Mediterranean, sir?'

'No.'

'*Centaur* was off Toulon with a convoy last October,' Fitzjames said. 'Seven gunboats came out and had a go at us – a dozen miles offshore and in a howling *gregale*, sir, making a good six knots into the eye of the wind. Three of 'em mounted a thirty-six pounder in the bows and pulled thirty oars apiece, the others mounted twenty-four pounders. We had the devil of a job to beat them off and only nailed one with a lucky shot before they gave up. We lost our mizen topmast and took three shot in our hull. If they could do that to a seventy-four, what'd they do to a brig-sloop mounting eighteen pounders?'

Honeyburn nodded. 'I concede your hypothesis. A twenty-four pounder can send a ball through two feet of solid oak at half-a-mile range. Go on with your proof, Mr Fitzjames – lame me with arguments, as Shakespeare says.'

'Well, sir, if what Mr Sholto was telling me is true that coast's a lee shore more often than not. It stands to reason they wouldn't build a sailing-vessel at Cap Breton when the prevailing wind would stop her from putting to sea.'

'Very well. And furthermore?'

'Furthermore we've only to consider what Charlotte's told us – Mademoiselle de Coulanges, that is. Those wagons, with the men and the timber and a dozen of what could have been guns.' Fitzjames's dark features were flushed with excitement in the lamplight. 'It'd take them months to build a twelve-gun sloop at Cap Breton even if they've got a dry dock there, which is about as likely as carronades in a cock-boat. No, sir – they could build twelve gunboats in a tenth of the time. Look at the way they were building 'em in every little port on the Channel when Boney was getting his precious invasion ready.'

Some of his excitement had communicated itself to Honeyburn. Here, surely, was full vindication of his past actions.

'I believe you are perfectly right, Mr Fitzjames,' he said. 'I should have thought of that myself. And there's another thing – the canal to connect the Cap Breton harbour with the lagoon. Suppose the gunboats to have been constructed on the shores of the lagoon. They would be launched upon it and –'

'You've hit it, sir!' Fitzjames broke in, snapping his fingers. 'They'd put to sea by way of the harbour, which is probably too small to take 'em all at once. It's all Lombard Street to a China orange! You must –' he amended this quickly – 'if I may suggest it, sir, this ought to be told to the naval authorities as soon as possible.'

'That is of course. I intend to report it at Orio.'

'They might let you off a wigging.' Fitzjames's schoolboyish grin vanished under his senior's cold regard. 'I beg your pardon, sir,' he said hastily. 'I was only thinking we'll get some credit for bringing important information. And sir,' he went on, 'if you were to mention that much of it is due to Mademoiselle de Coulanges –'

'Naturally I shall do so,' Honeyburn said with a touch of impatience. 'Whoever commands at Orio should then be the more ready to assist me in my requirements, which will be suitable accommodation for mademoiselle until such time as a passage to England can be arranged for her.'

'There might be some female who'd come with her in *Cracker*,' ventured Fitzjames, but without much hope.

'Impossible,' snapped Honeyburn.

But he felt very grateful both to his lieutenant and to the French girl. Between them they had provided what he regarded as incontrovertible evidence to support his theories and justify his actions. A patter of footsteps on the deck overhead was followed by the striking of two bells of the first watch.

'And in this matter of Mademoiselle de Coulanges,' he began.

'Yes, sir?' Fitzjames interjected eagerly.

'You will please to find out from her – tomorrow morning, not tonight – everything she knows about this aunt of hers in England. Madame de Goursac was the name, I fancy. I need to know where Madame de Goursac is to be found. Make a note of that and of any other information you consider useful and let me have it before I go ashore tomorrow.'

'Aye aye, sir.'

'Mademoiselle will remain on board until arrangements

have been made for her ashore. Very well, Mr Fitzjames. Pray pass the word for my steward. – One thing more,' he added as Fitzjames rose and went to the door. 'If you can contrive some sort of – um – garment for mademoiselle to wear under that Spanish flag –'

'Yes, sir – of course, sir.'

Fitzjames, flushing with embarrassment, departed and left Honeyburn chuckling. Food and wine and the changed prospect for his report at Orio had restored his feeling of well-being. His wounded knee gave no more than a twinge when he stood up with the aid of the boat-hook to assure himself that the oiled-canvas package of dispatches was in the drawer where he had placed it; and Mr Trapp, arriving in his character of surgeon with the steward, was bidden to let the bandaging alone and have an extra strapping ready for the morning. When they had gone Honeyburn got himself unaided onto his cot and lay for a while considering the phrasing of tomorrow's report and the action likely to be taken on it.

There was one British frigate on the Spanish coast, he remembered; Page at Portsmouth had named her, *Princess Charlotte*. All that was needed was for that frigate to anchor close inshore off Cap Breton (twenty fathoms half-a-mile out, he remembered) and pound the harbour to pieces with her 18-pounders. Or, better still, land a half-regiment of redcoats and destroy the gunboats. There could be little or no opposition – and that of course was why the French, operating in so vulnerable a position, had closed the road and kept what secrecy they could.

Cracker's gentle pitch and the swing of his cot were lulling him and persuading his mind from connected thought. *Princess Charlotte* ... an apt coincidence in the name ... young Fitzjames – a romance there? A fast-sprouting one if there was ... Cecilia Tuftoe ... there should be some credit in this Cap Breton affair for Henry Honeyburn, perhaps even promotion ... he might be wearing a new epaulette on his left shoulder when next he visited Mrs Tuftoe ...

On deck someone shouted four bells and the ritual calls of the lookouts were in Honeyburn's ears as he fell asleep: 'All's well – all's well!'

It was [illegible]
the [illegible]
brought [illegible]
week [illegible]
behind [illegible]
sail [illegible]
snail like [illegible]
that was [illegible]
The [illegible]
behind [illegible]
Gu [illegible]
for [illegible]
p [illegible]
once [illegible]
and [illegible]
under [illegible]
approached [illegible]
big [illegible]
on [illegible]
dark [illegible]
hid the [illegible]
headland [illegible]
sea [illegible]
Humphrey [illegible]
could [illegible]

V

Orio

1

It was two bells of the forenoon watch before *Cracker* sighted the diminutive port of Orio. The hours before sunrise had brought a restless and uncertain wind that eventually veered sou'-westerly, and sunrise itself had been invisible behind a canopy of low grey cloud. The gun-brig, forced to sail close-hauled under her reduced canvas, had made a snail-like progress across a choppy sea in gloomy weather that was very unlike yesterday morning's sunlit blue ocean.

The gun-brig's captain stood on his quarterdeck, balancing with some little difficulty to the rhythmic sway of *Cracker*'s movement. Mr Trapp, earlier that morning, had not only added extra support to his bandage but had also presented him with a walking-stick contrived from the outer end of a studding-sail yard, with a leather hand-grip and a leather-bound tip. Honeyburn had tucked this stick under his arm the better to use his glass in surveying the approaching coast. This was a different approach from the big sheltering bays of Santander and Bilbao he had entered on *Cracker*'s previous voyages. The long line of coast, dark-green below the level roof of purple-grey cloud that hid the hills behind it, was unbroken by any prominent headland and revealed only one narrow indentation at sea-level.

Honeyburn knew this must be the inlet of Orio because he could discern the shipping, a considerable number of vessels, clustered there close inshore. Lord Wellington, he reflected, must be confident of making a further advance very soon; for Orio, though providing a convenient temporary channel for troops and supplies to reach his army, was nothing but a shelterless anchorage, and a Biscay gale could render it unusable. Once San Sebastian was taken and the road to the French frontier opened Wellington would be able to use the fine harbour of Pasajes, but it was evident that his need to get San Sebastian into his hands was a very urgent one and the arrival of the convoy with reinforcements a prime necessity. Today was August 20th, he remembered. The convoy, assuming it had sailed as ordered at noon on the 18th and made a normal passage, should reach Orio on the 24th or 25th; though a persistence in the Channel of the fair wind *Cracker* had experienced would mean a shorter passage and an earlier arrival – as early, perhaps, as the 22nd.

He put the glass in his pocket and propped himself with the stick while he surveyed the gun-brig's deck. Up for'ard Sholto, with three or four hands assisting and Mr Trapp contributing advice, was trying to improve the set of his improvised topsail on what was left of the foremast; the boatswain was dissatisfied with the arrangement and proposed to re-rig it completely while they were in Orio. Some of the duty watch were in the bows staring at the coast. Nearer to him, leaning on the weather rail between two carronades, Fitzjames and Charlotte de Coulanges were engaged in animated conversation. Charlotte had a pea-jacket of the lieutenant's thrown round her shoulders and had tied a red bandana kerchief – also Fitzjames's, presumably – over her head. They were very close together. Honeyburn frowned and fingered the folded paper in his pocket; it bore a note that Madame Marie de Goursac's present address could be obtained from the Société des Amis de la France in Highgate, London. It was a good thing, he told himself, that Charlotte would be left at Orio when they sailed for England.

Cracker was closing the land now and his glass showed him more details of the shipping; three or four large vessels at anchor, transports probably, and a three-master that looked very like a frigate. A large brig under all plain sail was heading away westward along the coast, for Bilbao, no doubt. There would be a good deal of coming and going between Orio and Bilbao just now for the transferring of stores and equipment for the army engaged in this crucial attack on San Sebastian. Honeyburn raised his voice.

'Mr Fitzjames! I'll have the colours and the private signal hoisted, if you please. – *Mademoiselle, venez ici, je vous en prie.*'

Fitzjames shouted for Timmis, who acted as signalman, and jumped to the flag-locker. Charlotte came quickly aft and dropped a curtsey in response to Honeyburn's bow. There was anxiety in the gaze she fixed on him as she rose, and he felt sorry for her.

'In a little while I shall be going ashore, mademoiselle,' he said gently. 'I shall see the port captain here and arrangements will be made for your accommodation in Orio. It should not be long before you sail for England suitably accompanied – some merchant-ship masters are accustomed to have their wives on board with them.'

'It is necessary, monsieur?' she said in a low voice.

'I regret, mademoiselle, that it is necessary.'

Honeyburn bethought himself of *Cracker*'s imminent berthing close to other vessels; Charlotte draped in her Spanish flag was an object to invite comment. 'I shall ask you to retire now to the cabin,' he added, 'and to remain there until I return on board.'

'I will do as monsieur asks,' she said dully. 'Monsieur has been very kind.'

She turned and went slowly below. Honeyburn watched her go, frowning. it was ridiculous, but he felt guilty at proposing to leave this child alone in a foreign port. Yet what else could he do? He resolved to make very certain that she was accommodated as comfortably as his small stock of golden guineas could provide.

Orio, as the gun-brig drew in towards it, looked singularly unprepossessing and a good deal smaller than he had expected. Below the grey clouds the dark hill-slopes ran down on either hand to a narrow river-mouth where a quay, with some dilapidated buildings on it, flanked the entrance. There was considerable activity on the quay and boats were plying between it and the anchored ships, but the town – if town it could be called – lay some distance up the little river. No boat came out to meet the incoming vessel and Honeyburn, having given his orders for taking in sail, took *Cracker* in past two Spanish coasters and dropped anchor a cable-length from the only British ship in the anchorage, which was the frigate. As he had expected, she was the *Princess Charlotte*. As soon as the gun-brig was riding to her cable he got the packet of dispatches, summoned Gomez, and managed with some assistance from Fitzjames to get himself and his walking-stick into the waiting cock-boat.

A boat-load of men in green uniforms (Portuguese infantry, Honeyburn thought) were being landed at the quay amid a good deal of shouting and more green uniforms were ranked untidily on the crumbling flagstones. The men from the boat formed with the rest, a bugle brayed untunefully, and the detachment marched away towards the village as Gomez helped his captain up the ruinous steps to the quay. Honeyburn leaned on his stick and looked about him. A dozen or so of rough-clad men, local fishermen by the look of them, stood farther along the quay staring at the shipping; outside the smaller of the only two buildings that boasted roofs two red-jacketed soldiers were sitting on a bench with glasses of wine in their hands – cavalrymen, judging by the three horses tethered to the wall; the larger building, which had the look of a warehouse, had a small Union flag suspended above its doorway. He turned to Gomez.

'I'll repeat my orders,' he said. 'Make your way to the village yonder, seek some reliable person, and find out if there's some place – a nunnery, perhaps, or a gentleman's house – where Mademoiselle de Coulanges can be taken in to reside for a week or more. It will be paid for, of course. Report to me here.'

'Aye aye, sir.'

Beyond Gomez's tall figure as he rolled away on his mission Honeyburn could catch a glimpse of the village a quarter-mile up the valley. It seemed to be no more than a huddle of tumbledown shacks. He limped towards the building that displayed the Union flag, encountering as he reached its doorway a young officer, wearing the tall shako of the Hussars, hurrying out.

'Port captain?' he repeated in response to Honeyburn's inquiry. 'That's Captain Brooker, ain't it? You'll find him in there –' he jerked a thumb – 'and still sober, this time o' day. You from the ship just come in?'

'Yes.'

'Any news of the thirteenth and twenty-fifth?'

It took Honeyburn a moment to recall that these were the regiments embarking at Portsmouth. 'They're on their way,' he said.

'Thank God for that. You'll have dispatches, no doubt, and I'll be riding with 'em when you've seen Brooker. Old Nosey will be damned glad to get 'em.'

The Hussar flipped a finger to his shako and passed on in the direction of the wine-shop, as it appeared to be. Honeyburn went into the warehouse. which smelt strongly of decaying fish, and was confronted by a Marine sentry guarding an inner doorway that had no door in it. The Marine came to attention and stepped aside, and he passed into a gloomy stone-floored hall one side of which was piled to the dirty ceiling with casks. Casks with planks resting on them formed desks for two clerks and a larger table for the big man wearing the two epaulettes of a naval captain who lounged in a chair behind it. Captain Brooker was talking to a plump young man in lieutenant's uniform who stood beside the table, on which were two bottles and an empty glass. Honeyburn, his hat under his arm, limped forward and announced himself.

'Honeyburn, sir, commanding the gun-brig *Cracker*, from Portsmouth with dispatches.'

Captain Brooker looked him up and down without immediate comment. His large mottled face showed no welcome smile and his deepset eyes were hardly more than slits, so that he looked half asleep. When he spoke his voice, slow and hoarse, did little to counteract this impression.

'Your arrival was observed, Mr Honeyburn. By all appearance your brig has been in action.' He took the package Honeyburn was holding out and passed it to the lieutenant. 'Slit this open, Charles. Well, Mr Honeyburn? You were in action?'

'I was fired on by the guns of the fort on Cape Higuier, sir, and one shot took –'

'Cape Higuier!' The captain opened his eyes a very little. 'Correct me if I'm wrong, Mr Honeyburn, but that is surely some way off your course from Portsmouth to Orio.'

'By your leave, sir, I have a report to make that will explain the divergence.'

'I trust so, indeed. And you yourself were wounded?'

'My injury is the result of a fall, sir,' replied Honeyburn with some truth.

In mentally preparing his verbal report he had decided it was unnecessary to mention the encounter with the French soldier. The lieutenant had placed the opened package on the table and Brooker glanced briefly at the covering letter before tossing the enclosed packed to him.

'This to that army lout, Charles,' he drawled. 'Give it him yourself. He's to ride to the camp at Mendiz forthwith. Now, Mr Honeyburn,' he went on as the lieutenant left the room, 'let us have this report of yours.'

The sleepy voice sounded amiable enough but Honeyburn was conscious of uneasiness; he found Captain Brooker's narrowed eyes and veal-like complexion unencouraging. Nevertheless, he began his account with confidence that increased as he proceeded, passing perhaps a little quickly over the expedition through the dunes and dwelling more upon the information gained by the rescue of the French girl and its undoubted significance. The captain heard him – or appeared to hear him, for his eyes were closed – without interruption, leaning back in his chair with his hands clasped over his paunch.

'And to sum up, sir,' Honeyburn ended, 'all these things without a single exception point to one conclusion – that the French have built gunboats at Cap Breton for an imminent attack on the next British convoy.'

Captain Brooker's thick lips moved slightly, as if he smiled in his sleep.

'Ye-e-es?' he murmured, almost whispering the word.

He sat up slowly, filled himself a glass of wine from one of the bottles, and poured it down his throat at a draught. Then he resumed exactly his former position and seemed to be contemplating his clasped hands.

'Mr Honeyburn,' he said conversationally after some seconds, 'you speak the French language and presumably read it also. Do you ever read *Le Moniteur*?'

'No, sir.'

'That's a pity, Mr Honeyburn. It's the newspaper whereby the Emperor Bonaparte informs his trusting people of the great benefits he has in store for them. Some of us make a point of reading it.' The deep voice spoke gently, as if to a child. 'The issue of the fourteenth of July – a significant date, Mr Honeyburn, for the French nation – announced with much bombast yet another grand scheme. The region of the Landes, hitherto the most unproductive part of France, was to be made to produce. A gentleman by the name of Chambrelent – if I remember aright – was to direct the work. Men, machines, tools, wagon-loads of young trees, palisades for fencing the plantations, were already being sent to the region, Mr Honeyburn. Ditches and canals to drain the region were being dug, Mr Honeyburn.' Captain Brooker unclasped his hands, placed them flat on the table, and fixed his narrowed eyes on the man standing before him. 'All these things without a single exception, Mr Honeyburn, point to one conclusion – that the French are preparing to convert the Landes marshes into a forest.'

Honeyburn had heard him with a growing dismay. His own convictions were badly shaken and he was suddenly aware that he was staring at the captain with his mouth open. But the possibility that he and Fitzjames had made a wrong deduction from the evidence was still only a possibility. Take everything into account, and surely –

'That may be so, sir,' he said boldly. 'And yet the forestry scheme could be a screen for the plan I have suggested.'

Since the captain made no reply but continued to stare at him with his eyes slowly widening and his face slowly reddening, he went on, though with less confidence.

'At any rate, sir, having acquired this information I considered it my duty to –'

'God strike me down!'

Brooker's oath came in a startling roar that caused Honeyburn to jump and one of the clerks to upset a pile of papers. He continued with such vehemence that flecks of spittle sprayed Honeyburn's face.

'You prate to me of duty – you! By God, you need to be taught your duty! You sail with important dispatches for Wellington and you waste a day dawdling after some piddling fairytale about gunboats. You risk your ship without orders, you run her into danger by a piece of lubberly navigation and get her dismasted. You take on board a French wench –' this approach to poetry halted his vociferations for a second – 'and you have the bloody impudence to come here and talk to me of duty! By my living bowels, Honeyburn, if you were in my command – and thank God you're not – I'd see you broke for it!'

He paused to wipe his mouth with his sleeve. Honeyburn, propping himself erect with his stick, had managed to force his bony features into a rigidity as expressionless as a stone wall.

'Gunboats, forsooth!' the captain went on, less noisily but with no diminution of venom. 'You conceive, I take it, that a gunboat can keep the sea for days and weeks, thirty miles from land, in order to pounce on a convoy. You're a fool, Honeyburn, and you'll pay for your folly.' He stabbed a forefinger at the lieutenant. 'I shall report what you've just told me to their Lordships and add my annotations. That report will be taken to England by *Princess Charlotte* – she sails in two days' time. See that your ship's log agrees with it. You'll have to produce it at the court martial.'

'Yes, sir,' said Honeyburn woodenly. 'And my orders?'

'Orders? Hell and damnation, what d'ye expect? Take yourself and your damned vessel out of my sight and back to Portsmouth, and sail within the hour!'

'By your leave, sir, I can hardly do that. The necessary repairs to *Cracker*'s foremast –'

'God rip me open!' Brooker smote his forehead and rolled his eyes heavenward. 'What's the Navy come to, giving commands to old women? You'll sail the instant your repair's completed – d'ye understand that? Then that's all.'

'Aye aye, sir.' Honeyburn stood his ground. 'There's one thing more. The French girl, Mademoiselle de Coulanges. I have to find somewhere to dispose of her while she awaits –'

'I'll have nothing to do with your God-damned French girl!' shouted Brooker, now purple in the face. 'Drown her – rape her – do what you like with her, only get out of my sight!'

Honeyburn, feeling that his self-respect required him to make no response to this, turned about and began to limp towards the door. Two officers stood there, he saw. One of them was Charles, Brooker's lieutenant, and the other, a lean ruddy-faced man a little below middle height, he recognised as Captain Gardiner of the *Princess Charlotte*. Gardiner had been a friend and admirer of Michael Fitton since the latter's Caribbean days. Honeyburn had sufficient acquaintance with him to make him feel hot with shame that Gardiner should have heard Brooker's words. He was with difficulty maintaining his self-possession and could only manage a brief response to the frigate captain's hearty greeting.

'I've some business here,' Gardiner said, 'but it shouldn't take long. I beg you'll wait for me, Mr Honeyburn.'

Honeyburn mumbled acquiescence and passed out of the building into the fresher air of the quay. Sea and sky were grey under the heavy overcast of cloud and it was cool for a Spanish noon. Out beyond the masts and rigging of the anchored ships he could see *Cracker*, dwarfed by the big hull and three tall masts of the frigate lying near her; figures moved on her foredeck at the base of the foremast stump. He saw these things dully, for the brief interview with the port captain had left him shocked and sore – as much from the reversal of his expectations as from Brooker's rough-tongueing. He longed to get back on board the gun-brig and shut himself in his cabin. But there was Gardiner's request to be complied with and Gomez's return to be awaited; and in any case he had sent the cock-boat back to the ship.

The group of idlers on the quay were staring at *Princess Charlotte*'s boat, which was lying-off a stone's-throw from the steps. The bench outside the wine-shop was deserted and the three horses had gone. Leaning heavily on his stick, he went across to the bench and sat down, addressing the swarthy man who appeared in the doorway in two words: '*Una verra.*' The wine when it came was dark-red and rough to the palate, but two sips of it cleared his mind and the grim future unfolded itself before him: the slow and tricky voyage home, the summons to court martial, the accusations of neglect of duty and endangering his ship, the final dismissal from command or even from the Service. It was useless to tell himself that had his own interpretation of his collected evidence been accepted and eventually proved correct he would have been commended for his zeal; Brooker had rejected it with contumely and here in Orio Brooker was the senior naval authority. Honeyburn gulped the rest of the wine and sat gazing miserably out across the gloomy sea. An approaching footstep roused him to awareness of Gardiner's approach and he reached for his stick.

'Good God, man, don't get up!' Gardiner increased his pace and sat down beside him. 'Mr Honeyburn, this meeting's a pleasure. *Cracker*'s been in action, I see.' He nodded at the lieutenant's outstretched leg. 'And you got a knock? Not serious, I trust?'

Honeyburn, somewhat moved by this blunt friendliness after his recent treatment, muttered awkwardly that his wound was the merest scratch and that *Cracker* had come under fire from the Cape Higuier fort in drifting sea-mist.

'The fault was mine, however,' he added glumly. 'It was my navigational error that took her in half-a-mile from the cape –'

'Could happen to any of us,' Gardiner said quickly, with a covert glance at his companion's doleful face. 'The damned currents in this corner of the Bay will set you two miles off course before you know it.' He hesitated a moment. 'See here, Honeyburn. I couldn't help hearing Captain Brooker's farewell address – indeed, that bull-bellow would carry half-a-mile or more. I don't mean to pry, but when a man hears a fellow-officer told to rape or drown some young Frenchwoman –'

He stopped himself as Gomez came to a halt in front of them and knuckled his forehead in salute.

'Will you excuse me, sir?' Honeyman said, recalled to remembrance of Charlotte. 'This man has a report for me. – Carry on, Gomez.'

'Aye aye, sir. Put in a nutshell, sir, there ain't no place yonder fit for a young woman to stay in, let alone a lidy like mamzelle. A corporal o' marines, sir, 'e says them 'uts at Orio is full o' fleas and fever –'

He had found the corporal of marines, said Gomez, at the only large house in the village, which had been taken over as quarters by the port captain with a small staff whose one ambition was to leave it as soon as possible. Gomez's rapid survey of the village's other dwellings, leaky hovels inhabited by unwashed fisher-folk, had confirmed the corporal's opinion.

'And that's damned right,' supplemented the frigate captain. 'Even the army wouldn't use the place for billets. Wellington's got his forces encamped at Mendiz, five miles up the road to San Sebastian.'

The total failure of his plans for Charlotte de Coulanges made little impact on Honeyburn's spirits, which were already at their lowest ebb. At this moment he felt incapable of considering this or any other problem; for that he needed solitude and the privacy of his cabin. He set the tip of his stick on the stones and hoisted himself to his feet.

'I must get back on board, sir,' he said heavily to Gardiner. 'Hail *Cracker* to send the boat, Gomez.'

'Belay that,' Gardiner cut in, standing up. 'You'll pardon me, Honeyburn, but I've an alternative suggestion. When I can, I keep old-fashioned meal-times in the *Princess* and my dinner's due to be served in half-an-hour. I don't like eating alone. Pray give me the pleasure of your company. *Noli metuere*,' he went on quickly as Honeyburn hesitated. 'I confess I'm with child to hear about your French girl, but if you don't want to tell I swear I'll not press you, 'pon honour.'

From a post captain to a lieutenant the invitation was the equivalent of a command. Honeyburn tried to make his reply sound enthusiastic.

'That's most kind of you, sir. Of course I shall be delighted.'

'Then send your seaman back to the gun-brig. I'll see you're taken aboard after we've dined.'

Gardiner turned away to call his boat alongside the steps.

'You may hail *Cracker* for the cock-boat,' Honeyburn said to Gomez. 'My compliments to Mr Fitzjames and I'm dining on board *Princess Charlotte*. – Wait.' He had remembered something. 'Tell Mr Fitzjames that Mademoiselle de Coulanges may appear on deck, providing – um – providing she wears a pair of his trousers.'

'Aye aye, sir,' said Gomez, writhing his features in an attempt to conceal a grin.

The grin on the face of Captain Gardiner, who had heard the instruction, was unconcealed and his eyebrows had raised themselves a full inch. He made no comment, however, but offered his arm as Honeyburn, beside him, began to move haltingly towards the steps. Brooker's gibe concerning old women who held commands was fresh in Honeyburn's mind and the mental picture of himself assisted across the quay like a gouty matron was repellent.

'I thank you, sir, I can manage,' he said stiffly.

'This is an order, Mr Honeyburn!' rapped Gardiner. 'Take my arm.'

Honeyburn took it.

2

'Well, it's a rare yarn,' said Captain Gardiner. '*In nuce Ilias*, 'pon honour.'

His sharp blue eyes held something of astonishment as he regarded Honeyburn over the rim of his glass. Honeyburn met his gaze with a touch of defiance. When he had first sat down at the table in the frigate's spacious stern-cabin he had felt humiliated and resentful; spotless table-linen and deft white-coated stewards had pointed the painful comparison between himself, a middle-aged failure facing ignominy, and Gardiner, two years younger and a post-captain with a fine record. But Gardiner's sympathetic manner and an excellent meal had melted his glum silence, and the wine – a Portuguese *bairrada* far more mellow than the stuff he had drunk on the quay – had loosened his tongue. When the remains of the meal had been cleared away he had been ready, with the slightest of pressures from his host, to tell the whole of his story.

'Aye – an *Iliad* in a nutshell,' Gardiner went on, setting down his glass. 'But –'

'But you would not have acted as I did.'

'Possibly not. Michael Fitton would, though, and you're a disciple of Fitton's.' Gardiner waved the matter aside. 'I've some comments to make on your tale and one of 'em's more urgent than the others. You've lost a foremast and you're to sail as soon as possible. You don't carry spares but I do, and I've a mainyard lashed on deck amidships that'd make you a jury-mast. What d'ye say?'

'That's most kind of you, sir –'

'Good,' said Gardiner, standing up. 'It'll have to be fished and rigged and that'll take time. Give me leave for a minute and I'll have my lads tow it across to *Cracker* right away.'

His quick light stride took him out of the cabin. Honeyburn sat staring out of the stern windows. The southerly wind was holding the frigate bows-on to the land, and the wide inward-leaning windows showed a prospect of empty grey sea and darkly-clouded sky. Gardiner's kindness had warmed his heart, but there was no blinking the fact that beyond that northern horizon disgrace awaited him. Yet his spirits had stirred from the rock-bottom depths to which they had sunk an hour ago, reviving his native stubbornness, and he told himself anew that facts and probabilities combined to make his own interpretation of the activities at Cap Breton the right one.

'That's under way,' said Gardiner, re-entering the cabin briskly and sitting down. 'I doubt whether you'll be ready for sea tonight, though. If Captain Brooker don't like that he'll have to lump it.'

'You place me under an obligation, sir,' Honeyburn began.

'Rubbish. A word in your ear about Brooker. He mixes brandy with his wine, half a measure of each. If you'd reported to him a couple of hours later he'd have been mellow and you wouldn't have received the jobation you did. By the bye, Brooker's senior to me on the list. If you were thinking I might overrule him –'

'I hadn't thought of it, sir.'

'Well, I couldn't do so even if I wished to. *Majori cedo.* Allow me.'

Gardiner tilted the bottle, which still held a little wine, over his guest's glass. Honeyburn interposed his hand and shook his head; he was unfashionable in not liking to cloud his wits. The frigate captain emptied the bottle into his own glass.

'Now, then,' he said. 'Item the second – the French young woman. A gentlewoman, it appears. So far as I can see, Honeyburn, you'll have to take her to England in *Cracker*. I've my orders to sail day after tomorrow for Portsmouth and I daresay I've better accommodation in the *Princess*, but she'd be in the same case here, save that she'd be alone with two hundred men instead of with three dozen. Moreover, I'm taking an important passenger. A nob.'

'A nob?' repeated Honeyburn as he paused.

'Aye. General William Carr Beresford, no less. Lord Wellington's right-hand man. Hasn't been able to sit a horse since he took a bullet in the thigh at Salamanca and Wellington's sending him home to see a crack London surgeon. So your little *aristo* can't very well appear on board here. But I can't think of any officer more suited to act *in loco parentis*, Honeyburn, than yourself.'

'Thank you, sir,' said Honeyburn with a wan smile.

Gardiner, frowning at his half-empty glass, seemed to hesitate before he spoke again.

'Item the third and last – your theory of gunboats.' He looked up, his level gaze fixing itself on Honeyburn. 'You've staked your career on that and I'm afraid you've lost. I'll be quite honest with you, Honeyburn. *Primo intuitu*, the plan holds water. To attempt a smashing blow at the supply convoys is what I'd do if I were Boney's commander-in-chief in Spain – especially at this stage of the campaign. What you and your lieutenant and your mademoiselle sorted out between you all points to some such attempt being in preparation. The scheme for planting trees in the Landes might very well be a bluff, as I'm told the Yankees call it. So far I'm sailing in company with you. But there's one grave objection to your gunboats. How are they to know when the convoy is within reach of their attack?'

'They could be informed of the sailing-dates from Portsmouth,' said Honeyburn. 'I can give an instance of it.'

He told what Gomez had reported to him in Portsmouth a week ago: the careless talk in the tavern, the listening Spaniard, the Spaniard's flight. Gardiner nodded slowly.

'That's of course,' he said. 'There's no keeping these things secret. So the spy flits across Channel with his information. To Cherbourg, let's say. That's five hundred miles and more from Cap Breton. With fast mounts and plenty of relays waiting they'd have the information at Cap Breton before a convoy could arrive off the coast there. Given reasonable weather the convoy shapes a direct course to Orio so they could count on its passing a point between eight and ten leagues due west of Cap Breton. So far, good. But when, Honeyburn – when?'

Honeyburn was silent. He had unconsciously avoided thinking about this undoubted obstacle, though it had been at the back of his mind since his interview with the port captain.

'I've been five days beating to and fro to win clear of the Scillies,' pursued the captain, 'and before that I've taken the best part of a week tiding it down Channel against the sou'-westerlies. With fair winds a fast convoy might be off Cap Breton in as little as four days. With foul winds it could take as much as fourteen.' He shook his head. 'It won't do, Honeyburn. No gunboats I've ever heard of could cruise for a week that far off shore, which is what they'd have to do to catch their convoy.'

'That's what Captain Brooker told me,' said Honeyburn dismally.

'Well, he was right. Brooker was a good enough sea-officer before he took to mixing his drinks and was put on shore. He had *Sirius* in the Mediterranean and he's had experience of French gunboats. So have I. They're big craft for pulling-boats – have to be, with a long twenty-four mounted in the bows and thirty men at the oars – but they've no room for stores and water. Watch from shore, spy your prey, dash out and straight at 'em – that's their game.'

'I'm sure you're right, sir. All the same –'

'You're not convinced?' Gardiner eyed him quizzically. 'You've still got McCormick's bee in your bonnet, eh? See here, Honeyburn. Show me how Cap Breton can receive news that a convoy's going to pass thirty miles away within the next few hours, and I'll strike my colours and hoist yours.'

'A – a rocket fired by a French agent concealed on board one of the ships,' suggested Honeyburn feebly.

'And visible thirty miles away?' Gardiner laughed. 'I can do better than that. A lookout on Ushant and a chain of semaphore signal-stations – some hundreds of 'em – right across France to Cap Breton. No, no – it just won't do. Take my advice, my dear Honeyburn,' he added kindly. 'Forget your gunboats and remember your gun-brig. You've to sail her across the Bay and up the Channel with a jury foremast.'

Honeyburn nodded resignedly. 'And I should be on board her supervising its rigging.' He got to his feet, slowly because of his bandaged leg. 'I've to thank you, sir, for your hospitality and assistance –'

'Belay the speeches, if you please,' Gardiner interposed, rising. 'Time enough for those when the General's dining at this table. My instructions from Brooker are to have a boat at the quay for him at four bells of the forenoon watch on the twenty-second and I shall have everything on a split yarn for up-anchor and away.'

Honeyburn's wound had been paining him when he came on board the frigate but rest had greatly eased it. There was no companion-ladder to be negotiated and he walked out onto the after-deck unassisted. His suggestion that he should hail *Cracker* to send a boat was brushed aside by the frigate captain, who pointed out that *Princess Charlotte*'s boat was already in the water and the bosun's chair waiting for him. The bosun's chair had been rigged as the most convenient way of getting him on board, and by it, having exchanged a farewell handshake with Gardiner, he made a swift if undignified descent into the sternsheets of the boat. Gardiner, at the rail above, raised a valedictory hand.

'Look to see me overhauling you before you sight Ushant, Mr Honeyburn,' he called.

And that, thought Honeyburn as the boat pulled away, was more than likely. Ahead across the diminishing space of ruffled grey water he could see busy activity on the gun-brig's foredeck. The spare yard from the frigate had been got on board and laid alongside the bowsprit with one end towards the foot of the foremast stump, and Sholto and Fitzjames could be seen directing the rigging of tackles on the stump and the mainmast. The afternoon was well advanced; it was unlikely, as Gardiner had said, that the fishing of the jury-mast to the stump, the rigging of shrouds and stays and blocks and halyards – all of which must be ready to stand a possible Biscay gale – would be completed by nightfall.

There was a figure on the foredeck that he didn't recognise. White trousers, officer's blue coat, short stature – could it be some emissary of the port captain's awaiting him? Only when he was halfway to Cracker did he realise that this was Charlotte, and he was relieved to see her go quickly out of sight as soon as she saw the frigate's boat approaching. Fitzjames and Mr Trapp, the latter muttering anxiously about hembrages, hauled him in over the rail with the help of a shove from the coxswain and the boat pulled away for the frigate.

'The new spar's aboard, sir,' said Fitzjames, 'and we're almost ready to fish it.' He hesitated. 'Did the – by your leave, sir, are they taking action against Cap Breton?'

'We'll talk later,' Honeyburn said shortly.

Behind the lieutenant the small anxious face of Charlotte de Coulanges showed itself and he limped towards her, doffing his hat.

'Mademoiselle,' he said, 'I regret to tell you that no quarters can be found for you in Orio. I fear you will have to travel to England in this ship.'

'Monsieur!'

Charlotte's face was transfigured, her eyes wide and shining. She took a step forward.

'I must assure you,' Honeyburn went on, 'that I shall make every – good gracious!'

Charlotte had kissed him.

3

It was mid-morning of the next day, August 21st, when *Cracker*'s anchor was at the cathead and she could show her stern to the port of Orio. Darkness had fallen before the task of getting blocks and tackles on the jury-mast could be finished, and the wind that had sprung up in the night, a westerly strong enough to set the anchored vessels jerking at their cables, had prolonged the task when daylight allowed it to be continued. When at last it was done the mast, about two-thirds the height of the mainmast, could carry only main and topsail and the blocks for two of the the jibs; and to balance this lack of upper sails the mainmast had to do without topgallant and royal. A cast of the log as soon as she had cleared Orio showed that even with a fair breeze abaft the beam the gun-brig could do no better than six knots.

Honeyburn watched the coast of Spain diminish astern with mixed feelings. The hills above the shore were as cloud-capped and dark as they had been yesterday, as dark as his future, and he was glad to see the last of Orio. But he was sad for *Cracker*. It was astonishing to discover how fond of her he had become, how deeply he was touched by her crippled condition. This, his first command (now likely to be his last) had been the fastest of her class, a fully efficient little fighting-ship more than capable of tackling any enemy vessel of her force, as witness her triumph over the sixteen-gun privateer *Lexington*; now she was too slow to manoeuvre for a fight, a lame dog.

She still had her teeth, however. He patted the cascabel of the stern-chaser at his side and turned to look for'ard along the perspective of hooded carronades, eight on either hand. Before yesterday's daylight faded he had spent an hour, with Gomez to help him, assuring himself that every gun was in perfect trim. Yes, she could still bite, even though she could no longer run or chase and her captain was as lame as herself.

Honeyburn, using his stick, took a few paces up and down his quarterdeck. He was not so lame as he had been, thanks to his new bandage. Last night he had at length yielded to Mr Trapp's dogged insistence and the old bandage had been taken off with the aid of warm water, revealing a wound by no means healed but clean and healthy; so much so that Mr Trapp had announced that his captain was now condolescent. Since the Frenchman's bayonet had penetrated a little above the knee it had been possible, when a plaster had been applied, to secure the new bandage so that it allowed some bending of the leg. Making the most of this one spark of brightness in his gloom, Honeyburn took another couple of turns. As he limped round to face for'ard he was in time to witness a little drama up in the bows – in dumb-show, for the sounds of wind and sea prevented voices from reaching him.

The group of men standing there and critically regarding the new rig on the jury-mast included Fitzjames, who had been commendably active in the work of fitting it. Charlotte de Coulanges stood watching them a few paces away; she wore the blue coat and white trousers belonging to the lieutenant and his red bandana was knotted under her chin. She walked forward and lightly touched Fitzjames, whose back was towards her, on the arm. He turned with a start, took a step backwards, and bowed slightly, with his hand to his cocked hat. A few words passed between them and then

Charlotte turned away with a little shrug. She came slowly aft and went below without looking at Honeyburn, and her face wore a puzzled frown.

Honeyburn frowned too. What he had just seen ought to have pleased him but instead he was saddened. He recalled the conversation in his cabin over the evening meal last night. His expurgated account of the interview with Brooker had been given and he had cut short Fitzjames's hotly expressed indignation and incredulity by pointing out that the main objection to their gunboat theory – the impossibility of the French knowing when a convoy would arrive off Orio – was insuperable. Fitzjames could find nothing to say to that, and Honeyburn had firmly closed the subject and turned to discussion of the arrangements for their passenger. Mademoiselle de Coulanges would continue to occupy the first lieutenant's cabin and her meals would be brought to her there; she would be free of the deck abaft the mainmast but would be desired to avoid the foredeck; she would at all times be treated with the deference due to a lady.

And then had come Honeyburn's unthinking mistake – unthinking although he had given thought to how he should phrase his next remarks.

'You'll forgive me, Mr Fitzjames, if I mention the attachment that appears to have sprung up between Mademoiselle de Coulanges and yourself – a somewhat rapid one, if I may say so, but natural enough in the circumstances. I'm now responsible for this young lady and I feel a word of caution is necessary. I'm not questioning your intentions, mind, but I'll ask you to bear in mind that mademoiselle is a lady of good birth, daughter of the Comte de Coulanges –'

'There's no need to go on!' Fitzjames had gone very pale. His interruption came in a high strained voice. 'You may believe it or not, as you wish, but I'd forgotten I was a bastard.'

'My dear lad!' Honeyburn was aghast. 'It never entered

my head – I had no intention –'

'I'm obliged to you, sir, for the reminder. Pray excuse me.'

And Fitzjames had risen and left the cabin.

Looking back on it, Honeyburn could not find that he had been altogether at fault; the chip on the boy's shoulder was too delicately balanced. And perhaps it was a good thing, on the whole, that the growing attachment had been nipped in the bud so conclusively.

The coast of Spain had dropped from sight some time ago and the circle of the horizon was clear and dark beneath the clouded sky. The steady wind, from a little south of west, raised transient feathers of white on the slight swell rolling in from the Atlantic and sent an occasional splatter of spray over the bow rail. A fair wind for Ushant if it held; a fair wind up Channel. *Cracker* was snoring along steadily enough under her low sail, though without her old liveliness. A week, perhaps, and his last voyage in her would be at an end and the sea of troubles would cast him finally ashore. Would they dismiss him from the Service or leave him on half-pay? It was as well that he had a little money put by, and a degree that might conceivably enable him to get a post as usher in some school.

That last idea woke no enthusiasm in him, however, for the past ten years had made him if not a true seaman at least a lover of the sea-life and of his ship. The roots he had torn up in abandoning life ashore and the scholastic profession had taken hold in the timbers of this little gun-brig. A jingle from one of William Wordsworth's lesser poems echoed absurdly in his mind:

Ah, happy, happy was the day
When to that Ship he bent his way.

Yes, he had been happy in *Cracker*; even on this voyage, fortunate in nothing except its favouring winds, he had had moments of pleasure, among them the meeting with Gardiner. The thought of Gardiner reminded him of the frigate captain's comments on the Cap Breton affair and his sarcastic suggestion of a chain of semaphore signal-stations across France, and he was still thinking of this when the boatswain came aft to report that a preventer stay had been rigged to the jury-mast.

'Mr Fitzjames,' Sholto added, 'he reckons it'd bear another light spar to carry a scrap of a sail, but I reckon not, sir. It'd bear a flag, maybe, but that's –'

'Deck, there!' came the hail from the mainmast-head. 'Two sail broad on the stabb'd beam, sir.' Then, after a brief interval, 'Ah, 'tis nobbut a couple o' barca longas, sir.'

'*Eureka!*'

Honeyburn shouted the word so loudly that Sholto took a step backwards and the man at the wheel jerked his head round to see what had happened. Their captain was limping towards the companionway as fast as his legs and his stick would carry him.

'Mr Fitzjames!' he yelled over his shoulder as he went. 'In my cabin, if you please!'

Recollecting this pivotal moment afterwards, Honeyburn was convinced that the light that had flashed upon him was the result of a three-point coincidence, the subject of his own thoughts linking simultaneously with Sholto's remarks about a spar and a flag and the lookout's identification of the barca longas. He often speculated, then, as to whether he would have received enlightenment had those three things been separated by longer intervals of time. For the present, however, he was concerned only to put this new idea to the test. Fitzjames found him sitting bolt upright at his cabin table, his gaunt face wearing a rapt expression.

'Sit down, Mr Fitzjames,' he said sharply, 'and recall the barca longa we accosted off Arcachon three days ago. Tell me what you remember of her.'

Since last night's conversation the lieutenant's manner towards his senior had been strictly formal, though it showed no sign of resentment. He answered slowly and a little stiffly.

'The barca longa, sir. Out of Arcachon according to her skipper though two of the hands said she was from Cap Breton. A long way off shore for a fishing-boat.'

'Just so. She was in fact on or near our course to Orio, which was approximately the course that would be followed by any convoy from England. You agree?'

'Of course, sir.' Fitzjames frowned, staring at him. 'But she was merely a fishing-craft, carried no guns –'

'Never mind that. Anything else about her?'

'Well – she was lowering a spar when we overhauled her. I heard the skipper tell you it was for an experiment with a new sail, though he didn't sound very certain about it. I remember thinking a light spar like that wouldn't take a sail unless they rigged proper stays.'

'But it would take a flag, Mr Fitzjames. A large red flag, let us say.'

Fitzjames sat up suddenly, his grey eyes alight. Honeyburn went on before he could speak.

'Captain Gardiner jokingly suggested a chain of signal-stations from the Channel coast to Cap Breton, to convey the news of a passing convoy by semaphore. The idea is preposterous, as he well knew. But why not a chain of signal-stations across a few dozen miles of sea?'

'The barca longas!' Fitzjames almost shouted. 'By God, sir, I believe you've –'

'Get the chart,' his senior interrupted peremptorily. 'And the pencil and parallel rulers. We can put this to the proof at once,' he added as the lieutenant complied. 'I'm no great mathematician so you'll please to monitor my calculations. First, though, your estimate of the height of that barca longa's mast with the additional spar hoisted.'

Fitzjames paused in unrolling the chart to consider.

'She had a tall mast,' he said. 'I'd say the total height would be well over fifty feet.'

'We'll call it fifty. Five feet above the surface a man's horizon is distant three miles, at fifty feet above it's nine and a half. In reasonable visibility, then, we can say that a sizeable flag hoisted on that masthead spar could be seen – with a glass – from another vessel nine miles away. Agreed?'

'Agreed,' Fitzjames echoed a trifle impatiently. 'So it's perfectly clear that a –'

'We'll take this step by step, if you please. Now, then.' Honeyburn laid the rulers on the chart and took up the pencil. 'Here's our southward course already marked. Except in very bad weather a convoy wouldn't diverge more than a few miles east or west of that line. The shortest distance from Cap Breton to an interception of that line –' he placed a ruler – 'is a fraction more than nine leagues, twenty-seven sea-miles. You told me, I recollect, of French gunboats in the Mediterranean making – I use your own words – a good six knots into the eye of the wind. Would you say, on consideration, that you exaggerated their speed?'

'By no means, sir,' Fitzjames said positively. 'Thirty oars, remember, and they're built for speed.'

'Very well. Then gunboats from Cap Breton would take about four-and-a-half hours to pull out to a point where they could expect to intercept a convoy. The convoy's speed we can only guess at, I fear, but let us assume eight knots and allow five hours for it to sail to the point where the gunboats are to intercept it.' He measured northward along the convoy course. 'Forty miles, and I mark the place – here.'

'And by God it's where we spoke that barca longa!' exclaimed Fitzjames. 'She could have been cruising there on the lookout. Cap Breton could have learned the convoy sailing date – the first one, before they postponed it –'

'Wait,' said Honeyburn.

He was as excited as Fitzjames but he was determined to finish the working-out of his confirmatory plan. He ruled a pencil line from his mark to the little cross of the church tower that showed the position of Cap Breton on the chart, completing the third side of an elongated equilateral triangle.

'Fifty-eight sea-miles,' he announced, frowning doubtfully. 'They would need seven barca longas.'

'Not necessarily, sir,' Fitzjames said eagerly. 'Your nine-mile interval assumes a man seeing a flag at fifty feet when he's at sea-level. If these barcas had a hand at their mastheads – not up the spar, of course – they'd see it at thirteen or fourteen miles. We could establish the distance exactly by trigonometry –'

'I fancy we may do without that. Assume six vessels, beating back and forth or holding their stations along this line, the innermost in sight of Cap Breton and all of them keeping within signal-distance of each other. The outermost sights the convoy to northward and hoists her signal flag, the signal is passed down the line and Cap Breton has it in a matter of minutes. The gunboats –'

'They'd have their crews standing by and all on a split yarn,' cut in Fitzjames irrepressibly. 'Out they come, a dozen of them, and they're there straddling the route an hour before the convoy's due.' He brought his fist down on the chart with a thump. 'You *must* be right, sir – you've proved it.'

Honeyburn smiled and shook his head. 'We have proved, perhaps, that such a plan would be feasible. We have not proved that the French have adopted it.'

'But it's a near certainty that they have,' argued Fitzjames. 'Surely you'll put back to Orio and lay this before the port captain, sir?'

'No,' said Honeyburn without hesitation.

The idea had crossed his mind and had been instantly dismissed. It was easy to imagine Captain Brooker's reaction if the reprimanded gun-brig captain turned back from the homeward voyage in order to show him a pencilled triangle drawn on the chart. But another idea stirred somewhat uneasily in his mind and he was about to suggest it when Fitzjames, who was biting his lip and scowling, spoke the thought for him.

'If we could come up with one of those barca longas we'd have proof, sir. We'd make the skipper talk.'

'Ah!' Honeyburn nodded approval. 'That is a more likely

possibility than it might seem, Mr Fitzjames. For observe this. If our assumptions are all correct, Cap Breton will have received the news that a convoy sailed from Portsmouth on the eighteenth at noon. It's no more than possible, but the French may have their chain of signal-vessels out on their stations already. And we may intercept one.'

Fitzjames bent eagerly over the chart and ran his finger along their course. 'That'll be near midnight if we hold on,' he said, looking up with a frown. 'We're twenty-odd miles out of Orio and there's another fifty to sail before we reach the place you've marked for the outermost vessel.'

'But if I alter course, Mr Fitzjames, to head a trifle more easterly –'

'We'd cut the signal line nearer to Cap Breton and do it before nightfall,' Fitzjames finished for him. 'An excellent plan, sir, if I may say so. I suppose,' he added, 'these barcas would use a night signal – masthead lights – if they had to report a convoy after dark.'

'That is something we may be lucky enough to find out this evening.' Honeyburn paused. 'And a great deal, Mr Fitzjames, hangs upon our being thus lucky.'

'Yes, sir. I realise that perfectly.'

'Very well. You may give the order to alter course – 'Honeyburn considered the chart a moment – 'north-east by north.'

'Aye aye, sir!'

Fitzjames sprang up the ladder and a moment later his voice was heard giving the necessary orders. Honeyburn sat staring at the opposite bulkhead, conscious of a rapid deflation of his spirits. He felt *Cracker*'s slight sway as she bore more to starboard, and her gentle roll with the wind now dead astern, but the alteration of course only brought a growing doubt of its efficacy. Archimedes, he told himself, had some reason to shout 'Eureka' when he sprang naked from his bath; Archimedes had found both theory and proof. Henry Honeyburn, on the other hand, had nothing to shout about but pure theory, and the possibility of proof looked more remote the more he considered it. Even if (and what an 'if' it was!) matters fell out as his pencilled diagram had suggested and he sighted one of the signal-craft, how was his slow-sailing gun-brig to chase and overtake the barca longa? She wouldn't wait to be questioned. He might perhaps get within gunshot under false colours and then, hoisting his ensign, intimidate her with a shot across her bows –

He dropped his hands on the table with a thump and shook his head. He was building on shifting sand. Look at the thing squarely and there was not one solid fact to be seen. Two certainties there were indeed: that if he could produce no proof of his theory he was going to be disgraced, and that such proof was practically unobtainable. Well, he would stay on the new course; he had nothing to lose by it through *Cracker* might lose an hour or two. He bent over the chart again (his pencilled triangle looked less convincing now) and established his present position by dead reckoning, a simple task with no alteration of sail since leaving Orio and the wind steady west of south. It would be three or four hours before the gun-brig approached that most imaginary line of signal-vessels; in another dozen sea-miles she would bring Cap Breton, twenty miles away, on her beam. He rolled up the chart, and as he did so eight bells were sounded on deck, reminding him of the change of watch and his own decision to take the first dog-watch. He took his stick and climbed slowly to the deck.

Cracker was ploughing steadily on across a dark and empty sea, and the weather, gloomy and overcast though it was, showed no sign of worsening. Up for'ard the hands were clustered in talk, no doubt discussing the alteration of course. Charlotte, who was standing by the rail amidships, watched while Fitzjames formally handed-over to his senior.

'Very well,' Honeyburn said. 'And since I fancy it will darken early we'll sup early. Pray tell Mr Grattan, with my compliments, to start preparing the meal. You'll eat in my cabin, of course.'

'Thank you, sir,' returned Fitzjames with the ghost of a grin, 'but I'm invited to sup in the warrant officers' mess.'

The pleasure this gave Honeyburn somewhat lightened his inner gloom. From detesting Fitzjames he had come to like him, and this invitation marked his acceptance as a full member of *Cracker*'s little company.

'Excellent,' he said. 'I wish you *bon appetit*, Mr Fitzjames. Be so good as to ask Mr Sholto to come aft.'

The young man strode away, passing well clear of Charlotte and briefly touching his hat as he passed. The girl made no response but stood for some moments gazing after him before she turned to look towards the quarterdeck. Honeyburn could see her hesitating. She seemed to come to a decision and began to walk towards him with the evident intention of speaking to him, but the boatswain, trotting aft, passed her and she halted. Honeyburn told Sholto in a few sentences of his suspicions concerning the barca longas and his intention of catching one if he could. Sholto, wagging his head doubtfully, reckoned they might get a royal on the main and shake the reefs out of the spanker for a chase, but she'd be that hard-mouthed with such ill-balanced canvas that the helmsman'd never hold her on course.

'Nevertheless we'll try it if we get a chance,' Honeyburn said, feigning a confidence he was far from feeling. 'It will be some hours before we're likely to sight anything.'

When the boatswain had left him he looked for Charlotte; a little apprehensively, for he felt sure she had resolved to ask him the reason for Fitzjames's distant behaviour. To explain that the boy was the Prince Regent's bastard and ashamed of it was impossible and a disingenuous suggestion that Fitzjames might be tiring of this new friendship was equally so. He was spared this embarrassment. Charlotte had gone to her cabin.

Honeyburn began to pace slowly up and down his quarterdeck, his stick thumping regularly. Every few minutes he stopped to rest his wounded leg, though the pain it gave was now very slight and apparently not exacerbated by walking. His reflections matched the darkening afternoon. He thought of Cecilia Tuftoe, the only woman with whom he could ever think of sharing his future. He could not in honour – a man disgraced and futureless – visit her again to ask the question he had pusillanimously left unasked a week ago. Only a week! It seemed a year since he had ridden back from Wickham, since he had listened to McCormick's ill-omened theory on board *Crane* and allowed it to take hold upon him. He ought to have known better, but it was too late now.

He paused in his walk to look over the shoulder of Erikson, at the wheel, and check the course. North-east by north until he had performed this almost certainly fruitless search for barca longas and then he would have to head north-westward to regain his course to round Ushant. And though *Cracker* was now six leagues or more from the French coast it had to be remembered that with this wind it was a lee shore –

'Deck, sor!'

It was either Nolan or Driscoll at the masthead, and after his hail there came, for some seconds, no further shout. Honeyburn waited. A fishing-craft, probably. It was far too soon to hope for one of his hypothecated line of signal-vessels.

''Tis boats they are, sor!' came the shout from aloft. ''Twas after countin' them I was, an' –'

'Where away?' demanded Honeyburn.

'Stabb'd, sor, for'ard o' the beam an' headin' westerly.'

The shouting had brought Fitzjames running aft. Honeyburn thrust his glass at him as he arrived.

'Aloft, and see what you make of them,' he snapped.

Fitzjames sprang up the shrouds and on past the lookout, up the topmast shrouds until he could climb no higher. When, after a short pause, his voice reached the deck it cracked on a note of triumph.

'They're gunboats, sir!'

VI

Chance and Change

1

Afterwards, Honeyburn was proud to remember that his first thought was for his command. The instant after Fitzjames's hail had confirmed the imminent presence of the enemy his volley of orders, sharp and shrill, set the boatswain's call squealing. By the time Fitzjames had come racing down to the deck the hands were tumbling up from below and running to action stations.

'We were right, sir – all the time we were right!' panted Fitzjames, his dark young face alight with triumph. 'By God, I'd give a fortune to be by when Brooker hears –'

'How many?' snapped Honeyburn.

'Ten to the best of my judgement, but I wouldn't swear to it. They seem to be keeping a sort of formation, sir, five in line abreast and t'others astern of them.'

'How far distant?'

'Not more than five miles, and heading west. We shall cross their bows on this course – before they come within gunshot, I'd say. And there's no doubt about it, sir. *This* made it certain –' Fitzjames returned Honeyburn's glass to him – 'for I could mark a long gun in the bows of every boat. Spray-covers on, of course, but they could be twenty-four pounders.'

'Very well.' Honeyburn ignored the question that was apparent in his lieutenant's eyes. 'Go for'ard, if you please, and await my orders.'

Only when Fitzjames had gone did he allow triumphant realisation to rise in him like a warm flood, sweeping away his doubts and fears. This vindicated all his actions. But elation endured for no more than a moment. He felt the warm flood drain from him, and the cold fact of present emergency ordered his thoughts with icy clarity.

The signal had been passed to Cap Breton – that must have been three or four hours ago – and the gunboats were on their way to intercept the signalled convoy. The point of interception, which they would aim to reach before the convoy, was something like seven miles ahead of them; pulling almost into the eye of a steady breeze, that would take them considerably more than an hour. (Here Honeyburn spared a moment to consider the convoy's rapid passage; if they'd had those easterlies down Channel they could have done it – Gardiner had said as much.) The pressing need, for there was little time to spare, was for him to decide what action to take.

Turn away from the gunboats, head westward and try to find and alert the convoy? It was impossible. *Cracker*, beating against a head-wind with her inefficient sails, had no hope of outsailing the gunboats on their undeviating course; she would be boarded and taken, or pounded to splinters, before she so much as sighted the watchful *Crane*. Yet – somehow – the convoy had to be warned. Suddenly the parting words of *Crane*'s captain flashed across his mind: *If I catch the hint of a glint of trouble round goes the convoy and away to westward with every stitch set.* If McCormick had a capable lookout at his masthead the smoke and flame of a sea-fight would provide that 'hint of a glint' from more than seven miles away. And there was no alternative.

Honeyburn gulped as he made his decision. But the necessity for a plan of action left no time for dwelling on the inevitable outcome. The picture in his mind, of two ranks of five gunboats each, presented him with the germ of a plan. He hailed the masthead, asking how the boats bore now.

'Drawin' a mite abaft the beam now, sor,' came the reply.

'Big craft an' comin' up fast. 'Bout four mile, sor.'

To attack the gunboats, or to draw their fire, *Cracker* would have to put about and come back southward across their course. Very soon now they would be in sight from the deck and he could gauge his distances, but before then – He turned irritably as a hand was laid gently on his sleeve. It was Charlotte, her small attractive face alive with anticipation.

'*Qu'est-ce q'arrive, monsieur*?' she asked eagerly. '*Nous allons combattre, oui*?'

Honeyburn had no time for explanations and the sight of Charlotte had given him the final item for his plan.

'*Mademoiselle*,' he said imperatively, '*apportez-moi votre – votre* –' the French for 'skirt' eluded him – '*le drapeau espagnol*,' he finished.

'*Tout de suite, monsieur*!'

Charlotte scampered away. Honeyburn shot a quick glance round him. The men were at their stations by the guns awaiting his order to load and run-out. Close to him the crew of the stern-chaser stood watching him expectantly; there would be no action for them for a while.

'Peters, get the colours ready for hoisting and bend them to the halyard. Erikson, I shall put her about in a few minutes and you'll steer due south.'

The orders came crisp and confident. The tactics he was going to employ were crystal-clear in his mind. Charlotte arrived breathless with her bundle of red-and-yellow cloth and the Spanish colours soared up to the spanker yard-arm. In the same instant Honeyburn caught sight of the black specks far on the starboard quarter.

'Stand by to go about!'

Round she came – but so sluggishly compared with her old liveliness! – and the sheets were braced on the starboard tack. He had seen enough of the distant gunboats to tell him that if they held on his course would bring him across their bows at very short range.

'Mr Fitzjames! I'll have all guns loaded and run out, if you please. Port broadside load with grape, starboard guns and stern-chaser with ball. Man the port guns. – And you, mademoiselle,' he added in French to Charlotte, who was standing beside him flushed with excitement, 'will go instantly to your cabin and stay there.' Charlotte hesitated. '*Allez*!' rasped Honeyburn fiercely, and she fled.

The foredeck was a pattern of orderly movement. The wooden buckets with the slow-match smouldering in their rims were being brought to the six guns of the port broadside; Tubbs and Parkin, ship's boys, were running back and forth with the charges from the magazine where Mr Grattan, having doused his galley fire, was in charge behind the fearnought curtain; the hollow rumble of the gun-trucks ceased as the last 18-pounder was run out. Fitzjames's deep voice reported all guns loaded.

Honeyburn could see the gunboats plainly now, not much over a mile away on the port bow. His glass showed him the flickering movement of the oars; they were pulling thirty oars, he thought, and with odds of ten to one against her *Cracker* had no hope at all if the French succeeded in boarding. That must be avoided at all costs. On the other hand, he must come in close with his short-range carronades, for if (as Fitzjames had thought) the gunboats mounted 24-pounders they could lie half-a-league off and pound him without any effective reply from *Cracker*. Another thought struck him – and only just in time. To give the order 'Fire as your guns bear,' as he had been about to do, meant that all six guns would fire in turn at one gunboat. He hobbled for'ard along the deck as fast as he could go and halted to shout.

'D'ye hear there! We're going to cross the bows of five French gunboats. Number one gun will fire at the first we come to, number two at the second, and so onward. Number five and number six will fire at the last gunboat. If we get a chance we'll do the same with the starboard broadside.'

Someone shouted 'Hip, hip for Honey!' as he turned to go aft and there was a roar of cheering, swiftly quelled by a bellow from Fitzjames. Then there was silence, in which

Honeyburn's voice as he called the lookout down from the masthead and sent the 6-pounder crew for'ard sounded unnaturally loud. *Cracker* forged ahead in leisurely fashion across a dark sea under a darkening sky, a crippled lion heading into a pack of wolves.

Honeyburn, braced against the lee rail, heaved a sigh of relief. He could see all ten gunboats – they were half-a-mile away and almost ahead – and they still kept their formation of two ranks in line abreast, pulling steadily westward. They could have brought their ten 24-pounders to bear on him ten minutes ago and blown him out of the water had they wished, but he had counted on the uncertainty which the advent of a strange brig under low sail, wearing Spanish colours, would raise in the mind of the gunboats' commander. Moreover, this flotilla was dedicated to the destruction of an important convoy; to achieve it the gunboats would want to gain a position whence they could attack the convoy from windward, and gain it without alerting the convoy sooner than was necessary. The din of firing from ten 24-pounders might easily defeat their whole purpose, and their commander was likely to delay opening fire as long as he could.

But now Honeyburn could see figures casting-off the spray-cover from the gun in the nearest gunboat, only two hundred yards away. *Cracker*'s open gun-ports could hardly be ignored and they had probably seen the drifting smoke from the slow-matches as well. Peters had hitched the halyard to the rail with the British colours ready bent-on. He unhitched it and sent the colours soaring up as the Spanish ensign came down.

'Mr Fitzjames! You may open fire.'

He was not a second too soon. The bow carronade flashed and banged as *Cracker* came abreast of the first gunboat. He saw the water under the gunboat's bows spurt up in a dozen white splashes – just short. Number two gun did better. The hail of grape swept the second gunboat from stem to stern. She swung round, her oars in a tangle of confusion and the cries of the wounded rising as she passed astern. Number three fired high, but the flying balls caught two of the men who were working frantically to load their 24-pounder and hurled them into the sea. At the moment when the fourth gunboat was drawing abreast Honeyburn was spun round by the blast of air that accompanied a shrill crescendo screech and only saved himself from falling by a desperate push of his stick. The roar of the enemy gun came (he thought) from a gunboat in the second rank, and the shot had passed across the quarterdeck without striking anything. Before he had recovered himself they were past the fourth gunboat and his glimpse of her showed no damage from his carronade, but he was in time to witness the effect of the deafening double report from his two after guns. The fifth gunboat was raked by one or both, and the brilliant flash of an explosion in her bows told that one of the balls had struck a powder-charge as it was being handled into the gun.

Then they were past. Honeyburn yelled his order and the gun-brig came about on the port tack, heading back towards the disordered flotilla. The disorder was more apparent than real. Two of the gunboats were clearly disabled, but the rest were manoeuvring to bring their guns to bear. And the second rank of five had not retained the line-abreast that had enabled him to strike so effectively, but were irregularly placed, no longer under way but turning with flailing oars to lie bows-on to his approach.

'Starboard broadside!'

The order was hardly necessary. The hands who had manned sheets and braces as she turned had raced back to stand to the starboard guns. He could see Fitzjames and Sholto dashing from gun to gun to ensure their readiness, Trapp and the two boys standing by with the charges for reloading. In an instant of revelation he knew that he would never again see his deck like that. That *Cracker* had emerged scatheless from her first attack was due as much to luck as to the enemy's unpreparedness and reluctance to open fire, and there would be no escape for her this time. She was like a pugilist with very short arms who, having begun the fight with a flurry of blows at close quarters, had now to suffer inevitable punishment from a more powerful adversary with a much longer reach. As the thought fled across his mind it was ratified by a spout of white water that rose and fell close alongside. At the same instant a large neat hole appeared in the reefed spanker above his head. The double thunder of the 24-pounders made an enormous noise – loud enough, surely, to carry across ten miles of sea. And he was near enough now to give his carronades a chance.

'Mr Fitzjames! Independent fire as the guns bear.' To Erikson at the helm he added, 'Steer for the nearest gunboat and cross her bows at –'

A startling noise overhead cut him short, a twang as if a score of untuned harp-strings had been plucked by a brutal hand. A shot from ahead had struck the lee shrouds of the mainmast, parting them except for a few strands of cordage. Again the French had fired high, hoping no doubt to dismast him and board. If ever they boarded – Good gracious, Honeyburn exclaimed to himself, my sword's below in the cabin. And the immediate mental picture of himself hobbling about with a stick and waving a sword was so absurd that he was near to chuckling when the first 24-pounder ball crashed into *Cracker*'s hull.

The gun-brig lurched violently – she was struck somewhere amidships below the rail – but she held her course and almost at once her starboard carronades opened fire. Between the deafening explosions he could hear Fitzjames roaring orders to prevent all six guns firing at the nearest enemy, but all the same three of them chose for target the gunboat that had fired that damaging shot. She was hit at least twice, for as the smoke drifted clear he could see the white gashes opened in her hull right on the waterline. Three out of action –'

Five seconds later Honeyburn was dragging himself painfully to his feet from the deck where he had been flung by the shock of a second hit on *Cracker*'s hull. He found his stick and propped himself against the rail to stare at the doom confronting him.

No evening light penetrated the heavy clouds and a premature darkness hung above the slow-heaving surface of a leaden sea. It was so dark that the flashes of the enemy guns were blinding in their brilliance. They were grouped in a semicircle ahead of him, those seven gunboats. None of his own guns would bear on them and he was at the mercy of seven 24-pounders. There was a crash and a clang for'ard followed by shouts and screams, and he saw a great gap in the rail and a carronade flung on its side. A rending crack overhead – the mainyard, shot through, dangled from the slings with its canvas flapping wildly. The gunboats were firing as fast as they could reload and the din made it difficult to think. *Cracker* must be manoeuvred so that she could hit back. To starboard, then. The order was on the tip of his tongue but it was never given. The rail to which he was holding was torn from his grasp and something smote him agonisingly in the chest, felling him to the deck.

Again he groped for his stick and somehow got up, conscious of sharp pain in his ribs but intent on getting the helm put over. There was no helm. The wheel had gone. Erikson was a heap of bloody rags in the scuppers. Before he had time to realise the magnitude of this disaster the gun-brig reeled as from the blow of a giant hammer. The mainmast leaned slowly, snapped the few strands of the wounded shrouds like cotton, and smashed down on the port side across the inactive guns. With only the sails on her jury foremast to influence her. *Cracker* turned slowly to starboard and began to drift with the wind astern.

The deck leapt beneath Honeyburn's feet as she was hulled again. The shock roused him from stunned immobility to a sudden blazing fury. They were smashing *Cracker*, his ship – pounding her to pieces. By heaven, they should see that she could still hit back! He must find Sholto, get tackles rigged so that she could be steered.

Before he had hobbled two paces a tumult of shouting broke out for'ard and he was aware that the guns had stopped firing. He saw one of the gunboats, her oars working like flails, come foaming alongside below the broken gap in the rail. Pistols flashed and banged – if once they gained a footing this was the end. The carronade that had been knocked over had been righted and Fitzjames and a crowd of hands were pushing it into the gap. It toppled over the edge, to smash clean through the gunboat's bottom. She sank in a matter of seconds but not before half the men in her had hurled themselves over the rail onto the gun-brig's deck.

From the confused *mêlée* that immediately ensued one man broke clear and came running aft sword in hand, yelling as he came. Honeyburn straddled his legs, braced himself, and swung his stick aloft. His sweeping sideways blow caught the upraised arm and deflected the downward stroke but he was reeling off balance as the Frenchman, snarling, whipped up his blade for the final cut. Then the man was gripped from behind – it was Gomez who had chased him – and slung overboard like a sack of rubbish.

'All right, sir?' panted Gomez, his eyes on Honeyburn's trousers and the spreading dark stain.

'Yes.'

His senses, preternaturally alert, seized the immediate circumstances. The cheering for'ard told that the boarders had been routed, but the French would surely try to board with more than one boat though coordination of attack would be difficult. His swift glance showed him the second gunboat coming up right astern and still three hundred yards away.

'She's bad 'it, sir,' Gomez was saying hurriedly. 'Mr Trapp, 'e says she won't last long –'

'The stern-chaser!' rapped Honeyburn. 'Come on!'

He got himself to the gun, stumbling across the débris of the shattered wheel. The 6-pounder was already loaded and run-out, the match glowing in its tub. He bent to peer along the barrel, dimly aware of a distant whistle-blast, long and shrill. Exultation flamed in him as he saw that the gunboat was dead in line.

'Stand by!' He waited while *Cracker*'s stern rose on a wave. 'Fire!'

Gomez pressed the match to the touch-hole and the gun roared and flew back on its tackles in a cloud of acrid smoke that prevented Honeyburn from seeing the fall of his shot. When it blew clear it revealed the gunboat apparently uninjured, her oars working fast as she turned away.

'Reload!' he shouted, furious at this attempt to escape him. 'Reload, curse you!'

'Ain't got no charge, sir,' returned Gomez without resentment. 'And they're drorin' off, sir – all on 'em. Look yonder.'

The flame of battle-madness died in Honeyburn and he felt suddenly cold and shaky. He propped himself with his stick and gazed round him at such of the surrounding water as could be seen across the wreckage of his deck. Gomez's outstretched arm indicated the cluster of long black shapes on the dark sea far astern. They were heading westward.

'Seven, sir,' Gomez said. 'We sunk two an' another's made off east'ard –'

So whoever commanded the flotilla knew his duty, which was to meet and destroy the convoy; he would spare no more time, risk no more of his boats, in order to finish off a helpless wreck. *Cracker* had done her best – but had it been good enough?

'Mr Fitzjames's respects, sir –' It was Sholto; he had come running aft with the carpenter at his heels. 'Both the boats has taken some damage, sir, but Mr Fitzjames reckons they'll float. We lost seven killed, sir. And there's Johns with an arm broke and Timmis with his head laid open –'

'Four foot in the 'old, sir,' the carpenter broke in urgently. 'Risin' fast and there's naught as we can do. Sinkin' under us, sir –'

His voice seemed to fade and the darkness to deepen.

Honeyburn reeled and saved himself from falling by an effort of will. Mr Trapp's voice returned.

'– that wound's opened up like I said it would, and if I don't get a leggiture on it –'

Honeyburn cut him short. 'Tell Mr Fitzjames –' He stopped; this was an order he alone could give and it needed the full force of his lungs. 'All hands to abandon ship!' he yelled. 'Away cutter and longboat!'

Sholto and Trapp scurried away for'ard and as Honeyburn began to limp after them Gomez grasped his arm to help him. Someone took his other arm. – it was Charlotte, he saw. She said nothing but he could feel her trembling. They skirted two shattered bodies, unrecognisable, lying in a black pool. Fitzjames, his face covered with blood, was working furiously with the boatswain and a throng of hands to sway out the boats; and under his feet the deck was taking on an increasing slant to port. By the gap where the carronade had gone overboard a length of slow-match, fallen from its tub, glowed and smoked.

'Leave me!' he snapped, pulling his arms free. 'Get mademoiselle into a boat, Gomez, and look lively.'

They went, reluctantly, and Honeyburn picked up the slow-match and hobbled to the hatchway. There was one last thing to be done.

He was two or three minutes below. When he hauled himself painfully up on deck again Gomez was waiting for him, to seize and half-carry him down the tilted deck and bundle him neck-and-crop into the sternsheets of the waiting cutter.

'Give way!' he shouted hoarsely. 'Lay to your oars and stretch out, there!'

As the boat surged away from *Cracker*'s side he twisted round on the thwart to gaze astern. Against the darkening sky the gun-brig's one remaining mast was a black oblique stroke; it would be a race between his slow-match and the water pouring into her hull.

The boats were a musket-shot clear and *Cracker* was still

afloat when the creeping spark of the slow-match reached the powder-charge he had laid on the floor of the magazine. A brilliant flash turned the twilight pitch-black and the thunderclap of the explosion set Honeyburn's ears singing. He watched while the flames rose from her burning timbers, watched their bright orange tongues sink and leave a raft of smouldering red on the surface. Then he could see nothing more. But whether because she had sunk or because of the tears that filled his eyes he could not say.

2

Shortly after nightfall the lowering skies of evening fulfilled their threat. The wind backed due south and blew half-a-gale, whipping the long Biscay rollers into broken seas, dashing the wave-tops into flying spray that repeatedly drenched the occupants of the boats labouring in the noisy darkness. It was impossible to keep in company on such a night and the longboat had quickly been lost to the sight of those in the cutter. When the half-conscious state in which he passed most of that stormy night allowed him to think, Honeyburn felt certain that she must have sunk.

Hour after hour he wrestled with the tiller to keep the cutter bows-on to the unending succession of huge black waves, but the action was automatic and he was continually willing himself to climb out of the deep apathy of weakness and hold in mind their very real peril. The weakness, he dimly realised, must be due to loss of blood. Mr Trapp had put a rough bandage above his right knee and he thought it had stopped the bleeding; its tightness was painful, as was the injury – perhaps a cracked rib – to his chest, but the pain was forgotten in the perpetual imminence of death.

For both *Cracker*'s sea-boats were totally unfit to face even a moderate blow. The mainmast in its fall had sent one of its spars through the longboat's side midway between keel and gunwale, and a 24-pounder ball had ripped away six feet of the cutter's rubbing-strake together with the plank beneath it, reducing her freeboard by a foot on the starboard side. In the first few minutes after the cutter was launched Mr Trapp had dealt as best he could with her damage by covering the gap with one of the bottom-boards and lashing two of the oars across it. This contrivance, its interstices plugged with rags and clothing, served to prevent a major inrush of water when she rolled but was of course very leaky, and baling by pairs of men in relays had been continuous from the first, Honeyburn's cocked hat serving as a second baler. The makeshift repair meant that the cutter, which normally pulled six oars, could only pull four; but – as Mr Trapp tersely commented – better four oars above water than six below it.

As for the longboat, Sholto had managed to get a tingle over the hole in her side (the 'sea-boat's box' contained material for a repair) but as this was applied inboard it was far from watertight and a seaman had been detailed to sit on it and keep it in place. This, and more, Honeyburn had learned in an exchange of shouts when the longboat had come alongside after the sinking of *Cracker*. Fitzjames had reported clearly and coolly. The gun-brig's dead included both ship's boys, who with Kraus, able seaman, had been killed by the ricochet of the ball that had struck the carronade. Two men had been crushed beneath the falling mast and one shot through the head by a French pistol. Erikson, killed when the helm was shot away, made the seventh. To a question from Honeyburn Fitzjames replied that his own wound was a light one – a pistol-bullet had grazed his scalp. In the longboat with him were Sholto and Grattan and eighteen men. He had thought it best, he added, to limit the number of hands in the cutter to thirteen because of her reduced freeboard.

It had crossed Honeyburn's mind that this last piece of forethought might have something to do with Charlotte de Coulanges' presence in the cutter. But he made a mental note to commend his lieutenant's capability in his report, if he survived to make one. He had given Fitzjames his estimated course to steer for Orio – sou'-west by south – and told him to keep in company if he could. Then the boats had begun their long pull into the night, with wind and sea rising, and after the first half-hour no more had been seen of the longboat.

It had been no easy decision, that course. A twenty-mile pull with the wind astern would have brought the two unseaworthy boats to easy landing on the French coast, if they could reach it before they sank; that might save thirty-nine lives but it meant surrender and imprisonment. The alternative, forty miles of hazardous struggle against wind and sea to reach Orio, had been taken because it was Honeyburn's duty to keep what was left of his command out of the hands of the French.

But often during that unending night he felt the cold clutch of doubt at his heart, and in the darkest hours before dawn saw *Cracker*'s last fight as a futile waste of lives. He visualized McCormick and his three troop-carriers sailing southward into the gathering twilight too far to westward to receive the warning he had tried to give; the gunboats achieving their surprise attack; *Crane* unable to cope with seven enemy vessels whose single powerful guns could bear on their targets from every angle; the disabling of the escort and the sinking of the convoy. His own ship would have been sacrificed to no purpose.

Seven of his people (he remembered with a pang the cheerful young faces of Tubbs and Parkin) had been killed who would be alive had he not resolved to fight, for he was sure that if he had not turned to engage the gunboats they would not have altered course to chase him. And now it seemed likely that the longboat was lost with another twenty-one men. The responsibility for all this was his alone, and the realisation of that recurred each time his thoughts escaped from the dull stupor that held them.

A grey dawn spread slowly out of the east, revealing a dark and tossing sea crested with white. Its growing light showed the occupants of the cutter to each other and brought a stirring of stiffened limbs and a word or two of muttered conversation. There had been little talk in the past eight hours except for the hourly order to change oarsmen; the men who were bailing had been relieved every fifteen minutes as nearly as Honeyburn could judge the time. The boat looked as though it belonged to one of the Thames-side hulks rather than to a King's ship.

Honeyburn, hunched and shivering in the sternsheets, was hatless and his wet hair was plastered across his forehead; the grim set of his bony unshaven face evinced his iron resolve that, this time, he would not disgrace himself by swooning away like an old woman. His wounded knee was stiff and painful, for Charlotte de Coulanges, huddled below the stern thwart, was sound asleep with her head on his thigh. Resting on his other thigh he held the boat's compass and his arm was on the tiller as it had been through all that long night. Side by side on the thwart facing him Gomez and Peters tugged patiently at their oars; like the rest of the hands they were stripped to the waist – Mr Trapp had commandeered shirts and jerseys to plug the gaps in his repair – and their faces and bodies were smeared with black powder-stains. Behind them half-a-dozen men were squatting amidships, two of them baling steadily, and up in the bows beyond the second pair of oarsmen Mr Trapp was sitting with his two patients. Johns's broken arm had been lashed firmly across his chest with log-line and Timmis's head-wound bandaged with a sleeve torn from the carpenter's shirt. Mr Trapp's customary loquacity had been in abeyance lately but now he shouted against the noise of wind and sea.

'Moderatin', sir – I say it's moderatin'!'

'Yes,' Honeyburn made himself answer.

Perhaps the wind had lost some of its strength, but the sea was still running high, the tall waves dashing their spray over the bows each time the cutter reared to climb them. The carpenter's contraption of oars and bottom-board and bulging cloths had held well and the water that surged back and forth in the cutter was not gaining, thanks to continuous baling. Next time she soared on a wave-crest he craned his neck to look round the circle of leaping seas but could see no sign of the longboat.

His movement had woken Charlotte. She gave a small apologetic cry when she found where she had been resting and gazed up at him anxiously.

'You have seen Georges?' she demanded.

'No, mademoiselle, but the longboat cannot be far away.' He found it difficult to formulate the French words. 'You are cold?'

Like the rest of them, she had been soaked to the skin all night, and the daughter of the Comte de Coulanges was not used to it as the seamen were.

'I am a little cold,' Charlotte said. 'But I am very –' she stopped short. 'But it is nothing, monsieur.'

'You are hungry. In an hour's time we shall eat, mademoiselle.'

It was no more than ship's biscuit that was served out from the sea-boat's box at six bells of the morning watch, but the food put new heart into them all and gave Honeyburn a resurgence of his failing strength. They had, he thought, made little progress on their course during the night; the head-wind and the necessity for devoting every effort to keeping the cutter from broaching-to had hampered them. But now, with the wind at last falling, they had a chance of making the Spanish coast before nightfall. He tried to shut out of his mind what would happen when he reported the loss of his ship to Captain Brooker at Orio.

Throughout the morning they toiled across the troughs and ridges of the grey waves under a grey sky, continually looking for the longboat but never sighting her. At noon a second issue of hard-tack was served out together with a drink from the barrico of water. No afternoon sun came to dry their drenched clothing and Honeyburn was thankful that this was August and the wind a southerly. Now that their immediate peril was past he was finding it increasingly difficult to keep mind and body in control, to stave off the overpowering impulse to relax into insensibility.

It was well into the afternoon watch when, scanning the horizon from a wave-top for perhaps the hundredth time, he thought he saw a dark speck appear and disappear far out on the cutter's port bow. He called Gomez aft, told him to take the tiller, and got painfully to his feet with a hand on the seaman's shoulder. An immense relief filled him as he saw that he hadn't been mistaken.

'The longboat,' he said loudly for all to hear. 'She's two miles ahead of us, fine on the port bow.'

He scarcely heard the French girl's '*Dieu merci!*' for he had seen something else, on the horizon and directly in line with the distant longboat. The sails thrusting above the dark bar of the sea's rim were surely a frigate's royals. Two minutes more and the topgallants were in sight. There could be no doubt of her identity. She was the *Princess Charlotte*, four hours out of Orio and homeward bound.

3

Captain Gardiner numbered among his ship's company a surgeon who was the most arrogant person Honeyburn had ever encountered. He was a small ferret-faced man named Boucher, with immense bushy eyebrows and a rasping voice.

'Not a word!' he snapped the moment Honeyburn, opening his eyes, saw him for the first time. 'I'll do what talking's necessary.' He picked up the hand that lay outside the coat's blankets. 'Pulse strong and normal. Precisely as I expected. You're fortunate in having me as your attendant. No other doctor would have risked the use of laudanum in the heroic dose. Forty-eight hours, the human corpus totally relaxed, and you're halfway to recovery, Mr Horniman. – Be silent!' he added with a fearful scowl as his patient opened his mouth. 'You may speak when I tell you to. You were about to ask me questions which I can answer without speech from you.'

He was short enough to pace up and down the three yards of the cabin deck without striking his head on the deckhead beams and he did so, with his hands behind his back.

'Your fifth rib is merely bent and not fractured. A plaster – applied by my own hands and therefore efficacious – will see that little matter out of the way in a day or two. Plaster is also adequate to seal the clean orifice in your knee. Through that orifice, by ill-advised exertion, you have contrived to squander an inordinate quantity of blood, Mr Horniman – be silent! – of which, as you are doubtless unaware, your veins contain no more than eight pints. Had you not fallen into my hands you might well have spent a month on your back. As it is, you will walk off this ship unaided when we reach Portsmouth in three days' time or thereabouts. I have satisfied you, I believe. If not, you may speak, but briefly.'

'My name is Honeyburn, not Horniman.'

'Immaterial.' The doctor waved it aside. 'Is that all?'

'I'm anxious to hear of two men of my crew,' said Honeyburn. 'They were wounded –'

'Your anxiety is misplaced, Mr – ah – Honeyburn, since they are in *my* care. A simple fracture of the humerus, an incision which has grazed the parietal. They are in the sick-bay.'

'Thank you – and for your skill in my own case.' Encouraged by a visible softening of the doctor's severity, Honeyburn ventured a request. 'If I might speak with Captain Gardiner when he's at liberty –'

'Your tongue.' Mr Boucher bent over to scowl at the obediently protruded member, laid a hand on Honeyburn's forehead and stepped back. 'I told Captain Gardiner I would inform him when I considered he might see you. He may have five minutes. Not a second more.'

He bustled out of the cabin. Honeyburn lay staring at the deck beams. The cabin must belong to one of Gardiner's lieutenants. By the swing of his hanging cot and the sounds of wind and sea he could tell that the frigate was flying over a moderate sea with a stiff breeze abaft the beam. Mr Boucher's harsh abruptness had helped to clear from his mind the cloudy after-effects of the drug and he could recall being assisted on board over the rail and trying to make some kind of statement to Gardiner, after which Gardiner and someone else had helped him down to this cabin. Since his memory took him no further he must then have collapsed; but at least (it was a great satisfaction to him) he hadn't this time made a public spectacle of himself.

Footsteps clattered on the ladder and Gardiner came in, closely followed by Fitzjames, who slipped past the captain to grasp Honeyburn's hand.

'How's it with you, sir?' he cried. 'Well, I trust?'

His brow from eyebrow to temple was crossed by a six-inch strip of plaster, and the look of concern on his dark handsome face hardly concealed its cheerfulness.

'Have you heard, sir?' he rushed on with hardly a pause. '*Cracker* did it! We –'

'By your leave, Mr Fitzjames.' The captain, who had frowned at this lack of discipline, spoke with some irony as he put the lieutenant gently but firmly aside. 'Mr Honeyburn, welcome aboard. I said the *Princess* would overhaul you before Ushant and I've kept my word. Boucher tells me you're on the road to swift recovery and by God I'm glad to hear it. You came aboard my ship looking like a corpse dug up a week after burial.'

Honeyburn stirred impatiently beneath his blankets. 'The convoy, sir. Fitzjames said –'

'Of course. You've not heard.' Gardiner glanced apprehensively at the door. 'That fellow gave me five minutes and he's a worse tyrant than Boney. *Brevis esse laboro. Crane* and the three transports came in to Orio at sunrise this morning, three hours before we sailed, and I had a yarn with McCormick. He was full of talk about a sea-fight he'd glimpsed south of Arcachon – gun-flashes and reports and the glare of an explosion. Of course he took his convoy away to westward at once, believing as he did that the French had been brewing some devilment on that coast. You should have seen his face when I told him of your – um – investigations and conclusions. "By the holy!" cries he. "'Tis lucky the Navy has one man of sense besides meself!" '

'And he'll report all that to Brooker,' put in Fitzjames gleefully. 'I'd like to see –'

'To Captain Brooker, if you please,' Gardiner interrupted with some severity. 'No doubt Captain Brooker will draw his own conclusions – as I did, Honeyburn. Naturally I knew nothing of your part in the affair until Fitzjames here told me, but your sailing-time from Orio fitted the circumstances and I was aware of your bloodthirsty inclinations.'

'Good gracious!' Honeyburn protested. 'It was the merest chance that we fell in with the gunboats, and I had no alternative –'

'Take my advice and don't say that when you make your report to their Lordships,' said Gardiner gravely. 'You acted on sound information despite your seniors' disbelief, saved the convoy and in doing so lost your ship. You'll have to face a court martial for that, y'know, but you don't need to fear the outcome. And let me add this. You were right and I was wrong. I haul down my colours as I promised.'

Honeyburn grinned feebly. 'I'll not accept your surrender, sir,' he said. 'At our last meeting my theory wouldn't hold water. But pray enlighten me concerning Mademoiselle de Coulanges. Is she –'

He stopped, startled by an outbreak of loud voices outside the cabin. One was the surgeon's, the other a bellow like an angry bull's.

'Out of my way, sir, confound you! I've seen wounded men before and I know when they're fit to see me!'

The door burst open and Mr Boucher was thrust in before a stout man in a red coat with a good deal of gold braid on collar and lapels. The surgeon, whose autocratic manner appeared unshaken, pushed both naval officers aside and bent to frown at his patient for a moment. He straightened, swung round, and flipped an imperious hand at lieutenant and captain in turn.

'Out!' he snapped. 'Out! You've had your five minutes.'

They obeyed, Gardiner with a nod and a smile for Honeyburn.

'You, sir,' continued Mr Boucher, scowling fiercely at the man in the red coat, 'may have three minutes, and you will take particular care not to excite this gentleman.'

'God damn me!' said the stout man, staring after him as he went out. 'Wellington himself couldn't come the Grand Cham better.' He turned to Honeyburn. 'William Beresford, sir, at your service. Like to shake your hand.' He shook it. 'Feel it an honour, sir. Heard the whole story from Gardiner and you're a hero, sir – should be in the Army.'

His heavy-jowled face was burned leathery brown by the sun, and while one of his eyes was preternaturally bright the was other glass, fixed and dull. He was standing awkwardly with his weight on one leg, and espying the stool which the surgeon used pulled it towards him and sat down with a grunt.

'General who can't sit a horse is no damned manner of use,' he said. 'Hope Baillie in London can do something for me. You'll soon be on your feet, Mr Honeyburn?'

'I trust so, sir.'

'So do I, so do I. Wish you full health and the commendation you deserve.' General Beresford rubbed his long nose. 'Had a word with Danvers at Orio. His troops were disembarking and Wellington will be damned glad of them. Their safe arrival was due to you, Mr Honeyburn. Thought I'd let you know I'll be mentioning that in my dispatch to the Secretary for War. Copy goes to your Admiralty lordships,' he added.

'I'm most grateful,' Honeyburn began.

'May help at this court martial Gardiner tells me you'll face. Court martial! Preposterous, damme! But enough of that or the Grand Cham will kick me out before I've had my say. This young Frenchwoman of yours, now. Charming – charming, eh?'

'I suppose so,' said Honeyburn.

The General winked. 'Don't mistake me, sir. I've two great daughters of my own and she reminds me of 'em. She's told me her story. Has to reach London and find her aunt, Madame de something.'

'De Goursac.'

'That's it. Well, don't see why I can't help. Take her to Compton, my place this side of Guildford. Cecily and the girls will look after her – take her up to London, find this madame aunt, see her settled. Be a field-day for 'em, damme! What d'ye say, Mr Honeyburn?'

Honeyburn took a second or two to consider; he had come to feel responsible for Charlotte. The General noticed his hesitation.

'Your friend Captain Gardiner will answer for my *bona fides*,' he said drily. 'Not to mention Viscount Wellington of Talavera.'

'Of course, sir, of course!' Honeyburn said hastily. 'It's just that I am – have been – *in loco parentis*, in a manner of speaking.'

'I'll take over your *locus* lock, stock, and barrel, never fear,' nodded the General. 'And – by God, here's that damned Bashaw back again!' He was on his feet when the door opened to admit the surgeon. 'You may spare your orders, my man!' he bellowed at him. 'I'm ready to march!'

He paused at the door to wink his one good eye reassuringly at Honeyburn and then was gone. Mr Boucher took no notice whatever of the General's words or his departure. He scowled in silence during his ritual of pulse and brow and tongue and then nodded pontifically. 'In one hour's time,' he announced, 'you will take a bowl of gruel which I myself shall prepare. With it you will take a glass of port wine. That will be your diet until this vessel is within twenty-four hours of berthing at Portsmouth.'

'I'd like a glass of wine now, doctor,' said the patient boldly.

Mr Boucher frowned. 'I will allow it. Doubtless you have a thirst.'

'I have something to celebrate,' said Honeyburn.

The day following this somewhat unfestive celebration the *Princess Charlotte*, with a westerly bringing up fair weather in her wake, made her landfall off Ushant and headed north by east for the Start. On that day Honeyburn received a visit from Charlotte de Coulanges. She was wearing a long silken gown; one of Gardiner's lieutenants, it appeared, had blushingly admitted possession of a *robe de chambre* and the captain had commandeered it for her. Its sprawling crimson dragons on a black background made her look pale but none the less (Honeyburn admitted the General's adjective) she looked charming. He was still young enough, he found, to feel glad that he was up and shaven, respectably dressed in a pair of Gardiner's trousers and his own uniform coat which had been cleaned and pressed.

The French girl was voluble in her thanks for his care of her and excited at the prospect of reaching London in the company of General Beresford's family. The General, she declared, was *très gentil*; at which Honeyburn, absurdly, experienced a pang of paternal jealousy.

'*Enfin*,' she went on after a moment's hesitation, 'it will relieve Monsieur Fitzjames. When we – when first I told my story Monsieur Fitzjames offered to escort me to London and help me to find my aunt. Perhaps, monsieur, you will be good enough to give him my thanks.'

'You should give them yourself, mademoiselle, surely.'

Charlotte tilted her small chin. 'It is difficult for me, monsieur. You see, he – he avoids me.'

She tried to speak coldly but the unhappiness in her eyes made Honeyburn uncomfortable, and he was grateful when the door opened to admit a steward with his bowl of gruel and Charlotte left him. Affection for both these young people had gown in him and he frowned as he spooned his gruel. Their love-affair was no concern of his; however, he wished he could see some solution to their troubles.

Whether or not Mr Boucher's treatment was responsible, he was so much recovered by the time the frigate was off St Catherine's Point that he was allowed on deck. It was a morning of light breeze and intermittent sunshine, and the *Princess Charlotte* was gliding smoothly past the green shores of the Island with a quartering wind and scarcely any list. Gardiner had provided Honeyburn with a stick to replace the one that had gone down with *Cracker*, and once he had been assisted to gain the deck he found he could manage to get about by himself.

Having with some difficulty shaken off Mr Boucher (whose manner was that of a proud inventor showing-off his latest creation) he visited Johns and Timmis in the sick-bay and found both seamen doing well; found the men of the gun-brig's crew on the mess-deck and spoke some words of commendation; and exchanged greetings with his three warrant officers, of whom Mr Trapp took up most of his time with a condemnation of Mr Boucher's medical treatment, which he described as 'obboslete'. When he hauled himself up on deck again the frigate was passing No Man's Land Fort with only three miles of busy water between her and the hill-clustered buildings of Portsmouth town.

Honeyburn had paused to rest himself at the foot of the mainmast when Charlotte came hurrying to him.

'Monsieur, they tell me I am to be ready to go ashore with *M. le Général*,' she said rapidly. 'There is little time and I must ask you a question. Perhaps you cannot answer it – I do not know – but there is no one else, no one, whom I can ask.'

She had clasped her hands about his arm and was regarding him beseechingly. Honeyburn, who knew very well what was coming, would have evaded it but there was no escape.

'You have seen how he – I mean George Fitzjames – behaves towards me since we left Orio,' she went on in the same low hurried tone. 'Before then we were – such good friends. I can think of no reason for his changing like this. If you know of one, monsieur, you must tell me – you *must*!'

Honeyburn was deeply troubled. If he told her that Fitzjames was a bastard of the Prince Regent he would be breaking the promise he had given at the outset of their acquaintance. Moreover, for all he knew this daughter of the old French aristocracy might count herself insulted by being permitted to associate with a young man of illegitimate birth. He was desperately seeking words in which to answer her when Gardiner's voice filled the deck like the roar of cannon.

'All hands to take in sail! Idlers below and lively about it! – *À votre cabine, mademoiselle, s'il vous plaît.* Rogers, lend Mr Honeyburn a hand to get below.'

So once again he was spared the attempt to solve the problem of a disjointed romance. The problem remained, however, and he devoted some thought to it when he was down in his cabin, without perceiving any solution.

It had passed from his mind an hour later, when he was standing at the rail of the moored frigate gazing across the bustling waters of Portsmouth Harbour. He could see *Cracker*'s old mooring, number twenty-two west. There were no vessels lying at the buoys; and there was one that would never return to lie there. Today was the twenty-seventh and the gun-brig had sailed on the fifteenth of August. It seemed incredible that so much of chance and change, hazard and folly, variation in his own fortunes and those of others, could have taken place in a dozen days. Wordsworth probably had more than one apt comment on the strange paths of human destiny but Honeyburn, not being able to call one to mind, made his own.

'Good gracious!' he muttered.

4

Lieutenant Henry Honeyburn came out from the chill shadow of the Whitehall doorway into the warm sunlight of a mid-September afternoon and stood at the top of the steps leading down into the cobbled yard. His white trousers were spotless, his blue coat and cocked hat were new, and he was wearing his sword. In a moment Lieutenant George Fitzjames, equally point-device, came out and joined him.

'Pray allow me, sir,' said Fitzjames, and grasped his commander's hand.

Neither of them smiled. The occasion they had just attended had been a solemn one. Below them, marching down Whitehall towards Parliament Street, a battalion of red-coated infantry was being cheered vociferously by a following mob.

'San Sebastian,' remarked Honeyburn. 'The news of Wellington's success is only two days old.'

'And *Cracker* had a hand in that,' said Fitzjames; he hesitated. 'Perhaps, sir, you've heard how – how Mademoiselle de Coulanges is faring in London?'

'I called at Madame de Goursac's yesterday. Mademoiselle is comfortably settled. Indeed, she told me that she would be here –'

Honeyburn checked himself. A carriage had drawn up outside the wide gateway and in it were two ladies fashionably dressed, one of them slim and the other stout and holding a white parasol. Fitzjames caught sight of them in the same instant.

'Excuse me, sir,' he said hastily, and went quickly down the steps.

Halfway across the yard he halted to doff his hat and bow to the girl who had got out of the carriage and started across the cobbles. Then he strode on and out of the gateway, to turn to the right towards Westminster Bridge. The girl, who had stopped to look after him with a hand to her mouth, turned and came running up the steps to Honeyburn, her frown changing to a smile as she came.

'I am late,' she cried breathlessly, 'but I see that all is well. The court martial did not, then, punish you for – for losing your ship.'

'I was acquitted, mademoiselle,' he said, smiling back at her.

He forbore to mention that the President, in handing back his sword, had spoken some heartening words of commendation for *Cracker* and her captain. Charlotte had suddenly become very solemn. There was something like fright in the hazel eyes as she raised them – by an effort of will, it seemed – to look at him.

'*Monsieur le capitaine*,' she said in a low voice, 'it is necessary for me to make confession to you. All this time, while you have given me such kindness and assistance, I have been deceiving you.'

Honeyburn, much puzzled, would have spoken as she paused but she stopped him with hand upraised and went on speaking.

'I told you that I was the daughter of the Comte de Coulanges. That was a lie. I am indeed the daughter of the Comtesse de Coulanges, but my father's name I do not know. It was an – an *affaire*,when the Comte was away –'

'Stop!'

Honeyburn spoke the word so sharply that the marine sentry in the doorway behind him turned his head with a jerk. He clapped both hands on the girl's shoulders and fixed her with a penetrating glare.

'*Ècoutez-moi*,' he said rapidly. 'If you wish your friendship with George Fitzjames to be renewed you will do precisely as I now tell you. Get into that carriage and drive towards Westminster Bridge until you overtake Fitzjames. Get out. Accost him firmly. And tell him exactly what you have just told me.' She hesitated. '*Allez!*' he rasped in his quarterdeck voice, and she turned and ran down the steps.

He watched her enter the carriage, which immediately drove away. From his stance he could see above the wall of the Admiralty yard, though only the upper parts of vehicles, and he watched the parasol come to a halt at the foot of the Whitehall slope. After a moment or two he discerned the movements of a cocked hat, whose wearer entered the carriage. Carriage, parasol, and cocked hat moved on and merged into the crowd of vehicles in Parliament Street.

Honeyburn sighed. Then he looked at his watch and went down the steps to limp briskly across the yard. At the gateway he turned to the left. He knew of a livery-stables at the back of Downing Street where he could hire a chaise. For this time the occasion warranted a chaise. He was going to put an important question to Mrs Cecilia Tuftoe.

GUN-BRIG CAPTAIN

Showell Styles

Lieutenant Michael Fitton, commanding His Majesty's gun-brig *Cracker*, was on his third voyage to Spain as escort to ships carrying supplies for Lord Wellington's army in the Peninsula when he came into direct confrontation with an American privateer, the *Lexington*. With this encounter he once again faced his old enemy George Clewes.

At 47 promotion still eluded Fitton, despite his many victorious sea-fights. For in the Admiralty he had an implacable enemy in Admiral Dacres. But even Dacres could not stop Fitton's next mission that was to lead him to the very centre of the fighting in the Peninsular War. It was a mission which was as dangerous to the heart as it was to the person. For it involved not only the Baron la Haye, political adviser to Joseph Bonaparte, King of Spain, but also his daughter Anne Brennier, with whom Fitton was already acquainted.

THE LEE SHORE

Showell Styles

The winds did not blow fair when they drove the crippled schooner *Nonpareil* on to the coast of Houat, a rocky island off the Breton Coast. Houat was to prove to be Lieutenant Robert Ring's lee shore – 'when a man's in trouble with small hope of getting out of it, he's on a lee shore'. Ring was a good seaman, and an unusual one in the year of 1810 at the height of the Napoleonic Wars since his mother was French. The knowledge of this language was to lead him into an alien world, a world of espionage and adventure, as he carried out a secret mission vital to three countries: England, France and Spain.

STELLA AND THE FIRESHIPS

Showell Styles

On the morning of 26 October 1800 Lieutenant William Bissell was lying on the deck of a French brig with a knife at his throat. On board his 74 gun ship *Montagu* an event that was to prove of even more importance to his life was taking place – the birth of Stella.

William Bissell was too outspoken to endear himself to the Naval Establishment and secure promotion. Yet he inspired great loyalty among his subordinates who followed him throughout his many exploits, culminating in a daring attack with fireships under the leadership of his rival-in-love Captain Lord Cochrane on the French fleet at Rochefort.

Drawing on historical records, Showell Styles has written another masterly tale of fast-moving action around naval exploits at sea at the time of Nelson.

GRUESOME TIDE

Eric J. Collenette

The time is Dunkirk. And Ben Grant is a seasoned submarine coxswain, experienced but as yet unbloodied in war. That is not to be long in coming. Taking with him fellow submariner Stoker Albert Finney, he volunteers for duty at Dunkirk and takes across a shuitje – a cross between a Thames barge and a small coaster. When he arrives at the beaches he is ordered to abandon her there and join Lieutenant Martingale, now in command of the destroyer *Brigand* after the death in action of his skipper. The job is no sinecure. For Martingale is no more a lover of following orders without good reason than is Grant himself, especially when matters of conscience are at stake.

THE MONDAY MUTINY

Eric J. Collenette

The war is over. But the Navy is still not at peace; it still has a role to play – tracking down illegal Jewish immigrant ships and trying to prevent their reaching Palestine. It is a role in which the men of the sloop *Condor*, including its coxswain Ben Grant, are mere pawns in a political situation over which they have no control. They are torn between their orders and their consciences when such an illegal ship is boarded.

Ben Grant has more to contend with than keeping the lid on a violent situation. And it takes Leading Sick Bay Attendant Monday, who rides the coxswain's back like a conscience, to bring matters to a head.

TARGET: BATTLESHIP

Barry Coward

The battleship was old, poorly armed and on her way to a refit. But first she had a mission – to see the convoy through to beleaguered Malta safely. In the enemy-dominated Mediterranean of 1941 the odds were stacked against them. Odds in the form of U-boats and Stukas.

There was more than mere ships and aircraft at stake. There were the people involved on both sides. The Captain of the battleship, and the woman he left behind in Alexandria; Ingemar Dormann flying Stukas from the Sicilian base; Katerina, the German nurse. Their emotions, their very lives were bound up in the fate of one small convoy that slowly steamed towards its destiny.

In this fast-moving novel of the war at sea, Barry Coward has written a gripping saga, full of dangers, dramas, tragedies and triumphs.